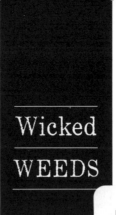

Wicked

WEEDS

A Zombie Novel

D1605958

Wicked
WEEDS

A Zombie Novel

Pedro Cabiya

Translated by Jessica Powell

[M]

Mandel Vilar Press

This book is typeset in Monotype Waldbaum. The paper used in
this book meets the minimum requirements of ANSI/N
ISO Z39-48-1992 (R1997). ∞

Publisher's Cataloging-In-Publication Data

Cabiya, Pedro, 1971-
  [Malas hierbas. English.]
  Wicked weeds : a zombie novel / Pedro Cabiya ; translated by Jessica Powell.

    pages ; cm

  Translation of: Malas hierbas.
  Issued also as an ebook.
  ISBN: 978-1-942134-11-4 (paperback)

  1. Zombies—Caribbean Area—Fiction. 2. Pharmaceutical industry—
Caribbean Area—Fiction. 3. Ethnobotanists—Dominican Republic—Fiction.
4. Haitians—Dominican Republic—Fiction. 5. Drugs—Fiction. 6. Man-woman
relationships—Fiction. 7. Noir fiction. 8. Science fiction, Latin American.
9. Speculative fiction. I. Ernst Powell, Jessica. II. Title. III. Title: Malas hierbas.
English.

PQ7442.C33 M3613 2016
863/.6

Printed in the United States of America.

16 17 18 19 20 21 22 23 / 9 8 7 6 5 4 3 2 1

Designed by Barbara Werden

Mandel Vilar Press
19 Oxford Court, Simsbury, Connecticut 06070
www.mvpress.org

Got no human grace,
Your eyes without a face.
BILLY IDOL

Pasó el tiempo y ahora creo
que el vacío es un lugar normal.
SODA STEREO

Dicen que soy
un desastre total. . . .
ALEJANDRA GUZMÁN

Warning

The album or scrapbook belonging to Dr. Isadore Bellamy is comprised of countless clippings, illustrations, photos, specimens, and texts. The curation of the present edition has focused on the presentation of those texts and has dismissed everything else.

By general consensus there are four textual categories, two of which, according to the experts, are not of the doctor's exclusive authorship. The manuscript has been classified and divided in accordance with these criteria of demarcation, *but only in the table of contents.* The main body of the volume respects and maintains the order in which they appear in the original. There are some who contend that such an order does not exist, that they are placed at God's whim—that is, by chance. Yet who can affirm that chance is not also a word, or many words, that we could one day learn to pronounce and in so doing become equal to God?

And so we issue a warning to the diligent reader, the one who will read in rigorous compliance with the page numbers: Your meticulousness and zeal will get you nowhere, for even following that path you will wind up in chaos. And chaos is a dark well where I cannot guarantee you'll find any comforting notions.

Others will conclude then, that the best approach is to use the compass provided by the table of contents and to read the book in the order established by the categories. And while, in practice, the chapters are scattered and intermingled, placed at unpredictable intervals (or in accordance with the brilliant but erratic doctor's fancy), these readers should fear not, for the table of contents will always deliver them to a safe harbor, telling them what goes with what. They will read all the things of one color and shape first, and the things of a different color and shape next, and so on, obeying the rule of like for like. This convenience, however, could be lethal. Because even incautious readers, naturally carried along by their own indolence, will not wish to veer from the path laid out for them by the judicious specialists, and they will, therefore, not read the album in the way Doctor Bellamy intended.

With tragic consequences.

PEDRO CABIYA
Grand Goave, 2010

Scrapbook
Contents

Records

Laboratory

Vacuus

Field Journal

Heartless

Transcription of the interrogation of Miss Mathilde Álvarez Koch, conducted by Detectives Jaime Almánzar Soto and Reynolds Rivera Sagardí.

JAS: Good morning, Miss.

MAK: [uncontrollable sobs]

RRS: Are you all right?

MAK: [unintelligible response]

JAS: Please, Miss Álvarez. . . . We know how traumatic this has been for you.

MAK: [disconsolate weeping]

RRS: Please, Miss, calm down. My colleague and I need to ask you some questions. Do you understand? You need to calm down.

MAK: Yes. . . . [hiccuping] Yes.

JAS: Are you feeling better?

MAK: Yes.

JAS: Would you like a coffee? Iced tea?

MAK: Coffee . . . Coffee, if you'd be so kind.

JAS: Of course. How do you take it?

MAK: What?

JAS: How many spoons of sugar?

MAK: I don't want anything. . . .

[silence]

JAS: Very well, Miss. As we indicated over the phone, you are here to offer your testimony regarding the events that occurred on the 24th of March 2009 on the corner of Arzobispo Márquez and Paseo de los Próceres, where Mister . . .

MAK: [disconsolate weeping resumes]

JAS: Miss . . . Miss . . .
RRS: This is impossible.
[sighing]
JAS: I'll call a cab.
[The interview ends.]

1. A Simulacrum / Qualia

If what the Gospels say is true, Lazarus must have felt something similar when Jesus ordered him to get up, to come out. Suddenly you abandon the darkness, the confinement, the stench; your lungs fill with pure air that smells like oats or myrtle, and all of your bronchioles get to their feet for a standing ovation; your muscles regain their elasticity, and your skin flushes with a heat that frightens off the cold; your belly is overcome by a tickling sensation, as when, as children, we used to get up in the middle of the night with a desperate need to pee—unless Lazarus, like me, was a zombie. Unless Jesus's "miracle" was a ruse, an incomplete favor, like the one they did for me. Because it's one thing to get up and walk, and another thing altogether to be *alive*.

For the time being we'll concede that Lazarus's was a true resurrection. What Lazarus must have felt, raised from the dead, and what I have for so long yearned for, I experienced two nights ago in a lively spot in the old quarter. The feeling, so concrete and real two nights ago, is losing its definition bit by bit, becoming blurred, difficult to retain, vanishing. That's why I've decided to write down my experience, because I harbor the secret hope that if I spill across the page all of the circumstances that led me to feel that I was alive (or to forget that, unfortunately, I'm a zombie), perhaps I could better detect the combination of factors that produced the fleeting miracle and discover the existence of a formula that would allow me to complete the process of resuscitation that my stupid family witch doctor left half finished.

Right off the bat I should clarify that, for a zombie, I think I'm doing quite well. I'm not a bit like those miserable types who spend years dressed in the rumpled overcoats they were wearing on that terrifying day when they awoke inside a coffin and, like moles, burrowed their way up through the earth of their gravesites; who have rocks and insect husks in the pockets of their threadbare pants; who grope the air in front of them with extended hands before taking each step, either because their eyeballs have dried up or because they've been slurped up by beetles and grubs; who walk like androids because their joints have frozen in a random position and they can no longer bend them.

If you saw me in the street you'd think I was alive. The minute I emerged from my grave I looked for, and found, the soap, towel, and tub of clean water that my executor had hidden among the headstones, and I gave myself a proper bath. From a backpack hidden behind the tub I pulled out a change of clothes and got dressed. My comfortable social position had allowed my family to buy a coffin of the highest quality, such that not a single insect had been able to make its way inside to nibble at my tender parts and no snake had invaded my anus to lay its eggs, as happened to one unfortunate fellow I know. For this reason my body is almost completely intact and more or less parasite free. One would have to examine me very closely to notice that anything was amiss. Expensive fragrances, lotions, and cosmetics (specially formulated for us, the living dead, by laboratories that long ago discovered this market niche and exploit it mercilessly), and all the other products of survival and camouflage to which I'm enslaved, guarantee me considerable freedom of movement. I can come and go as I please without raising suspicions or uneasiness among my fellow citizens. My life is such a perfect simulacrum that not only have I been able to graduate with honors in both pharmacology and chemistry, but they also love me in job interviews and offer me untold riches to accept their best positions. (If they only knew that they were hiring a creature from beyond the grave!) But make no mistake: I go about so paranoid and afraid of being discovered in the briefest moment of carelessness that any possibility of my establishing important emotional relationships with other human beings is irrevocably unavailable. In my interactions with others I'm incapable of going beyond politeness and allowing for an intimacy conducive to friendship. As a result, I'm an unsociable, solitary, and, so I've been told, extremely unhappy individual.

It's possible that my decision to enroll in the university might intrigue my readers and that they might find my choice of the aforementioned disciplines disconcerting. But I'd ask them: Is there a better way for a zombie to take advantage of his life in perpetuity than by dedicating it to the study of matter, the combined powers and limitations of the various elements, and the curative endowments of countless plants and animals in the hope of at last hitting upon the cure for his and so many others' affliction? Because, believe me, there are many of us, although the solitude that encircles my life would seem to argue just the opposite.

Well, it's not that my life is completely devoid of company. Once or twice a week I get together with other zombies in a sinister tavern in a housing complex on the outskirts of the city. Of course, each and every one of us at these periodic get-togethers would prefer to be somewhere else, sharing a table and conversation with real beings. If we come without fail it's only because we have no other alternative. Also, these occasions provide us with the rare opportunity to let our guard down; for a few short hours we're free of the tension occasioned by having to spend the day pretending to be alive. It's not friendship that brings us together, or even solidarity, but rather the common misfortune of not being totally dead—or totally alive, as the more optimistic of the zombies prefer to put it. As for me, I confess that sometimes I decide not to go because it seems obvious that my desire to overcome my limitations doesn't sit well with the others, and they see my plan to discover a remedy for our condition as a sign of arrogance. On the other hand, since I'm the best preserved of the lot, almost all of them either envy or despise me.

The owner of the establishment is one of the oldest zombies around and, certainly, the wisest. His name is Dionisio, and he's composed of a series of dried-up, dusty parts held together through a complex system of belts, straps, and Velcro that lend his remains a vaguely human semblance. Masked minions place him behind the counter every day at dusk, and there he spends the evening, immobile and ominous, like a symbol, one of those automatons that you activate with a coin in order to obtain a whole cloth prophecy. Dionisio is the only one I can talk to about my aspirations. He doesn't agree either, but his objections are not the product of petty grudges but rather of a refined skepticism. Our conversations are extremely beneficial because the elegance of his refutations forces me to constantly improve my research approach. I'll never forget what he said to me the first time I told him about my project.

"*Qualia.*"

"Qualia?" I asked, intrigued.

"To be dead," he explained in his gravelly voice, "has grievous consequences. The most obvious, of course, is the slow and distasteful decomposition of the body. In almost every survey done of our population, nine out of ten zombies indicate decomposition as the most troublesome symptom of their condition. They say this because they don't know, *they can't know*, that there's a worse one: the irreparable loss of qualia."

I still didn't understand. If Dionisio had been alive, he would, at that moment, have paused in order to take a long breath and resume his lecture, but, since he was a zombie, he merely paused. Habit, not hope, is the last thing to go.

"In brief, qualia is the living being's capacity to establish a connection between his experience of the world and the self."

"Yourself?"

"No, no, not myself—*the self*. Let's see. . . . A living person can understand that the things that happen *to* him, happen to something that *is* him, his self, the consciousness of being one's own self. If he feels joy or sorrow, if he's overwhelmed by beauty or by danger, he knows that he himself is feeling all of these things in such a way that he perceives the *attributes* of each."

"I don't understand."

"Of course not," sentenced Dionisio, "nor will you ever. I won't either. And this is the best evidence there is that we don't possess qualia."

"But then, how . . . ?"

"How can I speak with such authority about something I don't understand?" he said, cutting me off, then shrugged his shoulders. "I can explain it to you, but they are empty words that I've accumulated over the centuries, like someone who can recite perfectly a page written in a language he doesn't understand."

"What you haven't told me is what qualia has to do with my research. Whatever it is, it must not be indispensable. If I've gotten this far without it, achieving dead what very few ever achieve alive, it must be a superfluous characteristic, like breathing, which, by the way, I also haven't missed."

"That's where you're mistaken," said Dionisio, raising a fleshless phalange. "The quality of a thing is what indicates how that thing will affect you. And that information is crucial in order to make certain decisions and to recognize certain types of results. I'll admit that you're an intelligent zombie, the most intelligent I've met in a long, long time, but believe me, in order to achieve your goal you're going to need qualia."

I changed the subject without too much difficulty, and the evening took its course. I said goodbye quite late, but at the door it occurred to me to ask him one last question.

"Dionisio."

"Yes."

"If qualia is as you've described it, it seems to me that all of eternity would be insufficient for one of us to comprehend it as well as you have, if I'm to judge from your earlier exposition."

Dionisio didn't respond right away. The silence he allowed to grow between my words and his was a sign of reluctance. His face, inscrutable in its state of total decomposition, registered an incomprehensible expression. I stayed put.

"What do you mean?"

"Nothing. I don't know. . . . It just occurs to me that, in the same way that you've explained it to me today, someone must have explained it to you, once upon a time."

Dionisio twisted his lips and busied himself squirming under the strap that held his left shoulder in place.

"I was not mistaken when I said you were intelligent," he murmured, half closing his flashing ocular cavities. He finished fighting against the strap, laid his elbows atop the counter, and nodded his head. "Someone explained it to me. A long time ago . . . Someone who understood it."

RED

The color red is a neural response to the stimulation of electro-magnetic waves upon the retina; in other words, it's an idea, a figment of the imagination, a label that our brains affix to that part of the visible spectrum that exhibits the wave of greatest longitude. From red to violet, in descending gradation, our brains distinguish ranges according to the distance between the crest of one wave and the next. And in order to separate and indicate the experience of each of these ranges it invents a sensation: orange, yellow, green, blue—the labeling of each as arbitrary as the invention of a word to designate any given object.

A color is, in fact, a word, but a word so indelibly imprinted upon our experience of the real that we cannot imagine that it could be any other way. And yet it could be. . . .

We believe that colors exist in and of themselves, for themselves, but no. Colors, such as we perceive them, don't really exist. To the longitudinal range that we normally know as red, our biological architecture could have assigned that other optical experience that we call green.

We are capable of perceiving only the most minimal portion of the totality of the electromagnetic spectrum. We call this insignificant segment light. But what strange and indescribable color would x-rays be if we could see them? Or UHF waves? What color would the air surrounding us be if we could detect radio waves? What would the universe look like if we could see cosmic rays, the terrible light that illuminates the extremes of the spectrum beyond ultraviolet rays?

What occurs with colors also occurs with tastes, sounds, textures, smells. Our five senses are not portals through which we are conveyed to an external reality, but rather ports that receive stimuli utterly lacking in intrinsic qualities, that our brains adorn in accordance with evolutionary requirements in order to present them as Truth. But what really, then, is softness, blueness, sweetness? What is the real appearance of the world? What does "real" mean? Is it correct to speak of an "appearance"?

And yet, all of these fictions come to *me*. I receive them and they constitute *my* world. They define me. I exist insofar as it is I who experiences these lies. In the world everything happens to me. I am the collection of reactions and emotions aroused by the farce put on by my brain—like one who plays chess with himself. Wouldn't it be fair to say of love, hate, hope, pleasure, and, in short, of all emotions unleashed in answer to the existence of that supposed "exterior world" of which our senses speak to us—wouldn't it be fair to say of them the same thing we've said of colors? Is it possible that existence is not a feat of balance? Created from nothing, sustained by nothing, and sought by nothing, aren't we, every single one of us, but a single step away from dissolution? What separates us from the void?

Nothing separates us from the void. We carry it within.

We are the void.

2. A DILIGENT EXECUTIVE / LABORATORY NO. 3

I'm executive vice president of the Research and Development Division of the local branch of Eli Lilly. I'm in charge of twenty-eight plant chemists divided among five laboratories. I enjoy the confidence of my superiors and have a flexible schedule, and recently my name has been included on the list of executives with clearance to access confidential documents and the restricted substances stored in the vault on the ninth floor. I'm not a bureaucrat imprisoned in an inaccessible office; I labor away at the same lab bench as the rest of the employees, singeing my eyebrows over the Bunsen burner and graduating solutions into beakers like an apprentice. No one who has ever seen me at my place of work has ever seen me without my lab coat, cranking away.

I'm the only child of an affluent couple who, upon their deaths, left me all of their assets; in order to enjoy them the only thing I need to do is, well, simulate life. The fact that I'm independently wealthy doesn't make me soft; I'm no spoiled brat. I arrive early, before my coworkers. For a time I used the main entrance. The shift guard would open the door for me and bid me a good morning in a rugged voice. He was friendly and respectful. A few weeks later I became certain that he was a zombie. It wasn't the steel in his voice that gave him away, or the strong aroma of muskroot on his breath; I knew from the increasing tone of familiarity with which he began to treat me. It's relatively easy to fool a living person, but not another zombie. The guard had discovered my secret, and now he behaved as though some sort of brotherhood united us. I considered rebuffing him and, in so doing, regaining the lost distance between us, but I decided that it would be best not to arouse suspicions or to enmesh myself in gratuitous enmity. And so I began to use a side entrance near the dumpsters.

As they arrive to work, the members of my team proceed to their workstations in their assigned laboratories and take up whatever tasks were left over from the previous day. Each laboratory is dedicated to a specific project (the confidentiality clause in my contract prevents me from offering further details) divided into aspects or phases of analysis. These phases are executed at the different workstations by groups of up to three scientists coordinated by a lab manager who reports to me every two weeks. It is my habit, nonetheless, to supervise each station personally at least twice a week.

At first I tried to carry out my supervisory role from my office on the executive floor, but since in practice I was spending more time among pipettes than paperwork, I opted for a vacant table in Laboratory 3 and turned it into my base of operations. I know the names of all my chemists; I treat them all with equal courtesy and expect the same effort out of all of them. But I must admit that, while I maintain personal contact with every member of my team, it was inevitable that my prolonged presence in Laboratory 3 would lead me to fraternize more with the personnel assigned to that space—so much so that they were present on the night of my fleeting resurrection.

I don't know why I chose to invade Laboratory 3 specifically; perhaps because it seemed the least crowded. Perhaps it was because it's the only lab that's surrounded by glass partitions, like a showcase, presenting to anyone passing through the hallway a clear view of the experiments being carried out inside. Certainly, working without the visual impediment of four plaster walls does wonders to alleviate my claustrophobia, an unfailing acquisition for all of us who return to the world by means of slipping through the cracks in our own tombs.

On an ordinary morning, the details of which I no longer remember, I walked past Laboratory 3 on the way to my office. Although they were working busily, the lab's occupants paused, exchanged quick glances, and smiled at me cheerfully. I remember waving at them without stopping. That lab had the only team comprised solely of women: Doctor Isadore Bellamy, lab manager, Patricia Julia Cáceres, and Mathilde Álvarez. They had studied at the same North American university, taking the same classes and participating in the same symposiums, eventually graduating the same semester, although only Isadore had done so with high honors, in addition to completing a doctorate in molecular biology. They were inseparable.

The first thing I did when I arrived at my office that day was to take care of the bureaucratic aspects of my position, reviewing and processing pending documents, making and receiving calls, meeting with superiors and subordinates. Two or three hours later I stripped off my suit jacket, put on my lab coat, and began my rounds through the different work stations, listening to each lab manager's progress report. The last I visited was Laboratory 3, which had only one workstation, although there was room enough for two additional groups. From there I returned to my office and began to review my personal notes. My own research appeared to be completely stymied. It was at that moment that it first occurred to me that I could set myself up in one of the laboratories, given that my clerical duties required me to be in the office only three or so hours in the morning and that I dedicated the rest of my time to the labs. But, which to choose?

The question gestated alongside a detailed image of Laboratory 3 as I had seen it that morning when I'd responded to the three friends' greeting. In the spacious, glassed-in enclosure Mathilde was squinting into a microscope, examining a culture of liverwort cells dyed with lactophenol blue in order to reveal fungal elements, but her long blonde hair kept slipping down over the lens, and she'd had to tie it back in a hasty bun. When she'd lifted her hands to her head, her lab coat had opened and the hem of her shirt underneath had ridden up to reveal firm, steely abdominals and a pristine, flat belly button in which a gothic piercing glimmered. At another table, seated upon a tall stool, Patricia Julia was carefully pouring gel into a double electrophoresis chamber, her brilliant green eyes focused on her task, her bronzed, almost metallic complexion in marked contrast with her eyes. It was strange to see her so quiet, as she was, of the three, the loudest and most garrulous. That day she was wearing a short skirt; she had propped one leg up on the crossbars at the base of the stool, but the other leg was stretched out toward the floor, seeking stability, a perfectly smooth, sculpted column. Meanwhile, Isadore, standing next to Patricia Julia, with one hand on her hip and the other leaning on the marmolite table, was rereading a procedure. The hand at her hip caused her lab coat to open slightly, exposing a thin, floral-print dress that just barely managed to contain the flawless bulk of her jet-black breasts. Her almond-shaped eyes accentuated the roundness of her face, lending it an Asian air; her small ears sparkled with discrete earrings, and the muscles of her slender thighs stood out against her black skin each time she shifted her weight from one heel to the other.

No question, Laboratory 3 was the best choice, since, as one could appreciate from my extremely conscientious mental exploration, the team assigned to it used scarcely one-third of the total available space to carry out their work. In all likelihood, my decision was based on a simple impulse to take better advantage of underutilized laboratory space.

Business
Opportunities

Almost all of the most recent political exiles, industrialists and intellectuals who defected from Baby Doc's regime, took refuge in Arroyo Manzano, an inviting, cool, forested little hideaway in the hills overlooking the Isabela River five or six kilometers from Cuesta Hermosa. They built grandiose mansions and created, generally speaking, a highly insular and narcissistic community composed of the crème de la crème of the mulatto social ladder of the country they had renounced.

At first they didn't feel the need to socialize with their local counterparts. They were self-sufficient and arrogant. They lived off of ancient dues and interests; some were diplomats who made a living giving lectures sponsored by international organizations throughout the world. Others were successful international businessmen who had been able to retain their lists of clients and contacts.

Everything changed when these exiles had children and needed to send them to school. This second generation had to integrate into their host society, adopting their language and customs, thus expanding their social circles beyond the borders of the small redoubt of Arroyo Manzano.

The various and predictable social obligations incurred by the new brood forced the original fugitive group to incorporate themselves as well. The small community was infiltrated for the first time during birthday festivities to which they were compelled to invite their children's native schoolmates and during which, for better or for worse, the distrustful exiles struck up friendships with the mothers and fathers who dropped off their children and stayed to chat.

The small community's interactions with the external world became exponentially more complicated when their sons and daughters reached adolescence and young adulthood. For example, the illustrious families of Arroyo Manzano began to receive visits from girlfriends and boyfriends, and not always of the desired color and class. In no other place on earth are the rules of racial segregation stricter than they are in Haiti. The ignorant (the racists) will declare this a great irony.

In any event, the consternated exiles decided to take matters into their own hands and put a stop to the democratization of their progeny, which required them to cultivate the right kinds of friendships and to engender proper discernment among their children. And as they did this, they gradually shed their previous pride and discovered that, beyond their cultural and linguistic differences, they were linked to these other families through the delightful and all-powerful fraternity of money—especially the women.

They didn't always succeed; their children's friendships were not always to the exclusive circle's liking. In fact, some of those friends caused a visceral displeasure—friends like me, a daughter of immigrants who shared their nationality but not their social class, which is the same as saying their skin color.

Of course, none of this mattered in the least to Valérie, who paid less attention to the circumstances and twists of fate that divided us than to those that brought us together, especially within a society that was, in and of itself, already rather exclusive towards those of us from the adjacent nation. She was a yellow-skinned mulatta with green eyes and stubbornly frizzy hair. I was an unmistakable Ethiopian. I liked being with her because of her ease and lightheartedness. Nothing stressed her out and everything made her smile. She seemed to think that showing her teeth off to everyone was a kind of universal panacea. It goes without saying that she was a boy magnet.

I tended to be more obsessive and workaholic. When I was

with her I relaxed, forgot about my studies, and allowed myself the occasional indulgence in leisure; a lesson that, once learned, I never forgot, even when Valérie was no longer around. In any case, it never mattered; I always excelled beyond everyone else in all my premed courses.

The poor or mediocre students develop early on the ability to latch on to the more outstanding students as a means of survival within the university context. Timid and compulsive students almost always trade popularity for academic triumph. Seen from this perspective, our friendship was an impeccable symbiotic relationship. Although the initial reasons we were drawn together were, at first, opportunistic, in the end we were bound together by sincere affection. We were inseparable.

We always studied at her house; my neighborhood would have scared her to death. Her mother would have preferred a different best friend for her daughter, someone of considerably more noble appearance, but she appreciated my intellectual superiority and the positive influence I had on Valérie. Her name was Adeline, and she was a high-yellow Fula with ironed hair and a narrow backside. A high-assed Negress, as my mother would say—one of those who came to our country fleeing from Nevis and Virgin Gorda two centuries ago. Adeline, of course, would have taken offense at that, given that she traced her lineage, circuitously but with insufferable arrogance, back to a medieval family from Aix-en-Provence.

She couldn't stand to be spoken to in Creole and pretended that she didn't understand me when I did. She spoke Spanish if it was strictly necessary, but she exaggerated her accent in order to lend an exotic and snobbish air to her speech, and she used, without apparent justification, the Peninsular Spanish declensions. She was a source of fascination to her friends, high society white matrons from the capital. Spending time in the company of such a woman—black, exquisite, French, and wealthy—awoke in them a rare nostalgia, a melancholy for times they never lived through, and they imagined themselves part of an Algerian or Moroccan colonial tableau. But these are only guesses.

One evening Valérie and I were studying in the living room at her house when Adeline came in and asked us to move to the dining room table because she was expecting company. Valérie protested, not wanting to relinquish the comfort of the sofa and, especially, access to the television, without which she couldn't concentrate. I was happy to move, since I find tables better suited for studying. Sofas make me sleepy.

Having evacuated us, Adeline covered the end tables and the coffee table with all manner of hors d'oeuvres: pâté, cheeses, grapes, cured ham, cold cuts. There were also sweets and liqueurs. She stocked the bar with ice; set out wine glasses, tumblers, and highball glasses; and finally lined up two bottles of Grey Goose, one twelve-year-old Chivas Regal, a bottle of Barbancourt Estate Reserve, and several bottles of wine that had already been uncorked to allow them to breathe. She declined all of our offers to help and warned us not to even think of touching anything.

We were halfway through an endocrinology review when Adeline's friends, a select group of her most refined cohorts from the health club, began to arrive. Represented were the nearby and fluvial Cuesta Hermosa, the melodic Arroyo Hondo, the lively Piantini, and the distant and palatial Los Cacicazgos neighborhoods. These were followed by Bella Vista, Evaristo Morales, and Los Ríos.

Shortly thereafter, Adeline and her friends declared a quorum, officially opened the bar, attacked the trays, and got the party started. It was a boisterous group of eight. They made it impossible for us to concentrate. At first I found their conversation unbearable for its barefaced banality. It wasn't long, however, before the same shamelessness with which they discussed every trifling detail of their lives as though it were a transcendental landmark event in the history of the universe became irresistible to me, and I began to listen with rapt fascination. Throughout the course of the evening, as they diminished considerably the bar's provisions, their topics of conversation were the following:

Husbands

"Felipe is insufferable," declares Cuesta Hermosa. "You ladies have no idea how many times I've told that man to get a new golf bag, and he simply won't hear of it. I just die of embarrassment every time I have to go to a tournament with him. I tell him: Felipe, in these types of events winning is not the most important thing. A man like you can't neglect his appearance. Your golf bag is super old fashioned. And do you know what he says to me?"

"What?"

"That it's his lucky golf bag. That I should forget about it, he's never going to get rid of it."

"What you need to do," recommends Evaristo Morales, "is throw it away. Take out all the clubs and put them in a new bag. Throw the old one in the trash."

"Oh!" complains Arroyo Hondo. "If only mine were like yours and even took an interest in golf. But what can you do? These days he's all caught up in another blessed charity to help I don't know which nuns who have I don't know what foundation. I swear . . . It's as though he's forgotten he has children of his own! Tell me, at the rate he's going, what will be left for those boys to inherit? And in any case, you give the poor the things they need and what do they do? They sell it all. And the women popping out baby after baby. There's no help for them. The poor love being poor."

Children

"And who is Estefanía dating these days?" asks Bella Vista.

"Jan Luis," replies Los Cacicazgos, "the eldest son of the Menicuccis who own the Formosa Supermarkets."

"Jan Luis?" wonders Piantini. "But doesn't he have Down syndrome?"

"That's just gossip," chides Cacicazgos. "You know how people are. It was those rumors that broke them up the first time. . . . Okay, the boy does look odd, and he may have a speech impediment and a learning disability, but he comes from a good family and, most importantly, he's completely in love with my daughter. I told her the same thing. But no, no matter how much I tried to talk some sense into her, the little fool could not be dissuaded: she did not want to be a "retard's" girlfriend. I left her alone, because love can't be forced—until I found out that she'd been seen with a boy from Alma Rosa, perish the thought. I picked up the phone and called Jan Luis, I did. I stuck my nose in where it wasn't my business, but isn't that why we're mothers? I told him that if he really loved my daughter that he should come to her birthday party that Friday. It worked wonders. The boy arrived with a brand new BMW, a pink bow on the hood. Ah, such a nice touch. . . . They made up then and there and I told her to thank the Lord for sending her a man who loves her so much, because not even her father, in his entire life, has ever given me such a gift. I even gave them permission to take it for a spin—with the chauffeur, of course, because Estefanía doesn't have her license and the boy is forbidden to go anywhere near a steering wheel. . . .

Daily Life

"Today I needed to go to Prin to exchange a little dress I bought for Paola's baby, but, really, who can find the time?"

"The same thing happened to me, darling. I mean, imagine: I leave the house first thing to go to the gym, then stop off to pick up my evening gown from the cleaners. From there to Zara to see if I can find a belt to go with the shoes Sandrita brought me from Miami. By then it's two o'clock, I've got an armload of packages, and just ask me if I found the darned belt. And the 27 de Febrero in such gridlock that, if I didn't have Henry, the chauffeur, I'd have left the Mercedes right there in the middle of the road and walked home. Needless to say, I'm dead tired by the time I get through the front door."

Many other topics were discussed, but one thing led to the next until they all ended up discussing something about which they were of a single mind:

Maids

"They're all worthless."

"They're all thieves."

"It's so difficult to find a good one!"

"And when you do, it's so difficult to keep her!"

"So true. They're so proud that the littlest thing offends them."

"I've had good luck hiring evangelicals and Adventists. Although, of course, they won't lift a finger on Saturdays."

"Even the saintliest ones bring men into the house."

"And if she doesn't steal from you, then the men she brings in do."

"If I were to tell you . . ."

"And my God, how they eat!"

"The bad part about the ones that stay with you for a long time is that, bit by bit, they gain your trust and then they start to ask for favors and raises and loans. . . . I trade them all in for new ones at the end of each year."

"I had one that would try on my clothes. I discovered it purely by chance. Obviously, I had to burn everything in the closet. That same day I went to Miami to go shopping. You know how it is, one calamity after another."

"Oh, but I had one who tried to steal my husband. She'd make herself up every morning. Braided her hair, makeup, nails, tight little dress, like she was going to a party. And with that man, who's a tiger. . . . I said to him: No, in my house, the prettiest one is *me*. I sent her packing right then and there."

"I had one that started every day drunk."

"I walked in on one masturbating."

"My God in heaven! Where?"

"In her room—but tell me, is it, or is it not, my house?"

"Some of them stink."

"Well, to me they all stink."

"And what about the flood of children?"

"They have their first ones at thirteen or fourteen. . . ."

"Such ignorance!"

"I had one who couldn't even write her numbers."

"But, darling, I had one who signed her name with an X."

"And those names they have. . . ."

"So stupid."

"So ridiculous."

"Sugeidy."

Laughter.

"Primores."

Laughter.

"Leididí."

More laughter.

"Gracieusse!" said Adeline, giving a firm, curt clap. Her friends started laughing, buoyed along by the mood of the moment, but suddenly their laughter turned into shrieks of terror. Several dropped their glasses, which shattered as they hit the floor. The unanticipated screams served as prologue to an aghast silence.

We couldn't see what had happened from where we were sitting, so we got up and peeped in. We couldn't immediately identify the cause of the terror. We were entranced by the panicked ladies: petrified in various postures of fright, some covering their mouths with both hands.

But then we saw what they had seen.

It was a Congo so dark her skin glinted bluely. Her hair was a disaster, spiky and unkempt, as if she'd just had the restraints from an electroshock session removed. She was very short, with long arms and an abject face. She was barefoot and covered her nakedness with a scant yellow skirt and an old pink blouse. Both were far too small for her, as though a little girl had transformed into a woman overnight—as though she had never taken off the outfit someone had once dressed her in as a child. But the most terrible thing about her appearance was her eyes: blanched orbs that rolled in perpetual circles inside lidless sockets.

"Ladies," said Adeline, "allow me to introduce Gracieusse."

It was clear that some of the ladies were about to bolt. If they were unable to do so just at that moment it was because they were unsure as to which route to the door they could take without tripping over Adeline and Gracieusse.

"Your reaction is perfectly normal," Adeline continued, undaunted. "I've invited you all to my home under a suspicion, which I've been able to confirm this evening listening to you talk: not a single one of you is satisfied with your domestic help, nor do you harbor any hope that the situation might improve in the future. I can solve your problem."

The authority with which Adeline made her appeal relaxed the mood, although just slightly. Even the most cowardly among them considered staying to listen to what possible explanation Adeline might offer for having placed them in such a terrifying situation. Those who'd covered their mouths with their hands had not yet removed them.

"I'll cut to the chase," said Adeline in a serious tone accompanied by two concise claps of her hands, which had the effect of bringing Gracieusse instantly to her side. "Gracieusse doesn't eat or sleep. It's a good idea, however, to give her a bit of water now and then, once or twice per week, along with a handful of unsalted nuts. It's important that she never taste salt."

On the majority of faces the grimaces of consternation disappeared and were replaced by expressions of curiosity. Hands guarding mouths were withdrawn.

"Gracieusse does exactly as she's told," continued Adeline, "to the letter, even if the order she's been given jeopardizes her own . . . existence. She doesn't know how to differentiate. Of course, one must take precautions. After all, the smartest thing to do is to protect one's investment."

Cuesta Hermosa raised her glass of wine and took a sip. Piantini, Bella Vista, and Arroyo Hondo spread pâté on slices of bread. Los Ríos ate a grape. All eyes were on Adeline. No one dared ignore her presentation.

"Gracieusse has no sex drive. She has no idea what money is, and it doesn't interest her. Gracieusse, in fact, doesn't want anything, doesn't know anything, doesn't feel anything. Her sole purpose in life is to do what she's told."

Evaristo Morales, among those who'd screamed the loudest, stood up and approached Gracieusse, who, absently and acquiescently, allowed herself to be inspected.

"Boys and girls like Gracieusse come with their ears sealed with wax and a blindfold over their eyes. When they're delivered these seals are broken. The voice of the first person who speaks in their presence will be, henceforth, like the voice of God. Their face, the face of their lord and master."

"Do they come any taller?" asked Arroyo Hondo. "My ceilings are so high."

"I can get them in any size you want."

"Can their hair be done up?" asked Evaristo Morales. "Can they be dressed in other clothes?"

"Of course. I keep Gracieusse like this because she works in the washhouse out in the courtyard. It would be a waste of time and money to fix her up."

"How much?" said Piantini, who'd taken out her checkbook and awaited an answer, pen aloft.

It was difficult to understand what was said in the chaos of the ensuing hour and a half. Adeline registered the orders of her friends (who continually interrupted one another with childish desperation) in a notebook and stored their payments in a shoebox. She made out an invoice and receipt for each transaction. That night Adeline collected several hundred thousand dollars, issued in cash and check. Bella Vista asked twice if she could pay by credit card. The response was in the negative both times. One of the ladies had the nerve to ask where she got them. Adeline replied that her husband and his associates were in charge of that—that the less she knew about it, the better. Before bidding them good night, Adeline reminded them that she'd offer compensation for discrete referrals that resulted in sales. She did not specify the percentage she'd pay.

I was dumbstruck. Only later did I realize that I'd been witness to a kind of macabre Tupperware party. Valérie had gone back to studying as soon as she'd realized what was going on. I went back to the table and stared at her in such a way that she couldn't fail to notice my agitation. I needed to share it. She felt it, too, but not for the same reasons.

"Oh, I know, I know," was her only comment. "Such a shame. . . . She's always thinking about business."

I arranged to have lunch with Valérie the next day, but she didn't show up. Later, I learned that shortly after I'd left that night, her father, the retired Colonel Simònides Myrthil, had come home and hacked her and Adeline to death with a machete.

3. Eccentricities / The Only Answer

"Hmmm . . . ," said Dionisio, and the sound was the only indication that he was thinking, that he was pondering what I'd just told him; his body and face remained, of necessity, rigid. "Strange, very strange. Let's see: tell me again."

"I don't know how to explain it," I said. In the shadowy tavern, dozens of taciturn zombies drank and talked, occasionally looking at us out of the corners of their eyes. It was obvious that they envied the deferential treatment I received from Dionisio. "There's nothing to tell, really. They're eccentricities that I don't understand. Three months ago—no, four—I moved into the laboratory where they work. Before that, I saw them sporadically, during my supervisory rounds, but now we see each other all the time. If they ever have any questions, they consult me, and I help them. At the mere sight of me preparing the workstation for an experiment, immediately there they are, wanting to help me without even being asked. Sometimes they even argue amongst themselves; each one wants the other two to go away and let her help me alone."

"Hmmm. . . . Strange. Very strange."

"You're telling me? I've begun to suspect that they're simply looking for an excuse not to do their own work, but the truth is that they're very efficient and they've made more progress with their research than anyone else."

"In other words, it would not be right to fire them."

"Not in the least."

"A pity. That would have been a very expeditious solution."

"Dionisio, please. My wish is not to avert a situation that I don't understand, but rather to try to understand it."

"What else can you tell me?"

"Well . . . What do I know? For example, before, they didn't smell like anything, and now they smell all the time."

"They smell? What do they smell like? Of decay?"

"No! They do not smell of decay. They smell like—I don't know—flowers? Perfume. Fragrances."

"Hmmm. . . . And before they didn't?"

"No, before they didn't. Maybe every once in a while, but very rarely. Not like now. Oh, and they also dress differently."

"In what way?"

"They're showing more skin. . . . Now they prefer skirts, capri pants, sleeveless blouses. Their hair is perfect, and I never see them tying it up in a rubber band or with a pencil like before. . . . And their faces! They wear a lot more makeup now. All the time, as if they're on their way to a party."

"I see. . . . But they're not going to any party?"

"No. What party would that be? They stay in the lab working all day long. I don't know if they go out afterwards, but, in any case, they should be getting ready for that later, in the evening, not from the minute they wake up."

"Yes, that would be the most reasonable way to proceed. The most logical," said Dionisio. I'd never seen him so disconcerted. "But, what did you tell me about their attitude?"

"That's the worst part," I said, draining my glass. "As I told you, the three of them are best friends. But lately I've sensed a kind of tension in the air, sudden silences, silly quarrels over any stupid thing, whispered recriminations for things that must have happened a long time ago. It all puts me ill at ease, gives me a pit in my stomach, like vertigo, especially when they're very close to me, individually or together. I don't know how to describe it. You know me, so it should suffice to say that I can't even concentrate on my work."

"That's saying a lot," said Dionisio, and it seemed to me that he opened his eyes in disbelief.

"As I said . . ."

"Perhaps this has already occurred to you, I don't know, but if your work is being affected, why don't you move to a different laboratory?"

"I've considered that."

"And?"

"The only answer that I could give you is completely incomprehensible."

"Tell me."

"I don't want to."

"What? Why don't you want to tell me?"

"No, no. That's the answer. I don't want to. I don't want to leave. I wouldn't leave them for anything in the world, Dionisio."

"Hmmm," pondered Dionisio. "Strange. . . . Very strange."

Brainless I

Transcription of the interrogation of Doctor Isadore X. Bellamy Pierre-Louis, conducted by Detectives Jaime Almánzar Soto and Reynolds Rivera Sagardí.

RRS: Good morning, Doctor.

IB: Good morning.

RRS: Come in.

JAS: Please, have a seat.

IB: Thank you.

JAS: Can I get you anything? Coffee? Iced tea?

IB: Iced tea, if you'd be so kind.

JAB: Coming right up.

[Detective Almánzar Soto leaves the interrogation room.]

RRS: I'd like to take advantage of this opportunity to thank you for your cooperation and for the courtesy you extended us over the telephone.

IB: Of course. No need to thank me.

RRS: We know this is a difficult moment for you. Unfortunately, in order to prosecute the individual in custody we must gather all the evidence as soon as possible, all the statements—to be brief, everything we can gather with regard to the case—and turn it over to the public prosecutor's office so that they can move forward with the legal process. What I'm trying to tell you, Doctor, is that, at the end of the day, our job is the most thankless part of the entire legal machinery.

IB: I understand.

RRS: I hope so. Unfortunately, we didn't have much luck with Miss Álvarez.

IB: Yes, I know. She's . . . like that. Please forgive her.

RRS: If you cooperate with us, perhaps I will.

[Detective Almánzar Soto returns to the interrogation room.]

JAS: Here you are.

IB: Thank you.

JAS: Very well, Doctor, as we already told you over the telephone, you are here to give us your testimony with regard to the events that occurred yesterday, the 24th of March, 2009, on the corner of Arzobispo Márquez and Paseo de los Próceres, where Mr. . . .

IB: Yes, please, I know why I'm here.

JAS: Forgive me. Only a formality.

RRS: State your name for the record.

IB: Isadore Bellamy.

RRS: Your *full* name, if you'll be so kind.

IB: Isadore Xylène Bellamy Pierre-Louis.

RRS: And your nationality?

IB: I don't see what my nationality has to do with this, Detective.

RRS: [laughing] And here I'd held out hope that you'd be more cooperative. No need to be defensive, Doctor.

IB: My passport, Detective, is the same as yours. And if you purport to be a competent police officer who does his work thoroughly, you should already know that. But perhaps that's not what you really want to know, but rather my parents' birthplace, since mine, as you well know, is the same as yours. And if that's truly what you want to know, my answer remains the same: I don't see what that has to do with the investigation.

JAS: Very well. Of course, forgive us. Let's change the subject, shall we? Tell us, in what capacity did you know the victim?

IB: He was my boss. We were friends.

RRS: Friends?

IB: Friends.

JAS: Can you describe the type of work you did together, you and your boss?

IB: We worked for the Research and Development Division of Eli Lilly. He is . . . He *was* the executive vice president. I'm the lab manager. Our work consisted of proposing new lines of research for the creation of commercial compounds.

RRS: And what does that mean in plain English?

IB: If I were to put it in language so simple that even the most moronic could understand, I'd say that we were in charge of inventing new medications.

JAS: Who made these proposals? You?

IB: Sometimes. Others came to us from outside advisors. The vice president himself made most of them. To move forward with them required the approval of the board of directors, on which he also sat.

RRS: Quite a privileged position.

IB: I suppose so.

JAS: And were they approved?

IB: Almost always. Almost all of them.

JAS: What kind of medications were they?

IB: Stimulants, monoamine inhibitors, antidepressants—the kind of drugs taken by patients who are bipolar, schizophrenic.

RRS: Those kinds of drugs already exist. You have stated that your job was to invent new medications.

IB: It's true that medications that control the *symptoms* of these psychiatric conditions do already exist. In our line of research, we were looking to formulate compounds that *cure* these and other conditions and syndromes.

JAS: We understand that the victim worked in the lab although he had an office on the executive floor.

IB: The *victim* was a scientist of the highest caliber. He always spent the first part of his morning in the office: he took care of his administrative duties, putting the bureaucratic matters of the division in order. After lunch he'd put on his lab coat and work in the lab with us until six p.m.

RRS: You worked together? What I mean is, on the same projects?

IB: We helped each other, but everyone had a different project.

JAS: Him too?

IB: Yes. We never found out exactly what it was. It was a . . . secret project, so to speak. He accepted the help we offered only reluctantly. Once I managed to read his notes and glimpse his drawing of molecular models. Right away I knew that his research revolved around emotions.

JAS: How did you know?

IB: It was obvious.

RRS: Why?

IB: Because of his notes and the molecular models.

[laughter]

IB: The compound he was trying to stabilize was intended to adhere to the dendrites of the cerebral amygdala and restore the polarity of the axoplasm. The intercellular space is positive; the interior of the cell, negative. The greater the difference in electrical charge between the two, the greater the available voltage will be to create synapses. . . . I thought you didn't appreciate scientific pretension, Detective.

RRS: And you're not mistaken. Could you, in language so simple that even the most moronic of us could understand, tell us what the effect of this secret formula was?

IB: To electrify that part of the brain where the conscious self is manifest—like a defibrillator.

[laughter]

IB: You find it funny.

RRS: Forgive us, Doctor, it's just that, in our experience, the people who have need of a medication like that tend to look for a simpler method to electrify their brains. A slippery bathtub and a toaster or a hairdryer does the trick.

IB: Detectives, if you've had enough biochemistry for one day, I'll be going now. I have a lot to do and I still don't see how this line of interrogation could help the prosecutor lock up a confessed murderer.

JAS: Please, Doctor, don't go. Trust us. Everything serves a purpose. I promise that we'll pick up the pace. Tell us, Doctor, what was your boss like, personally speaking?

IB: Reserved. Extremely introverted. A control freak, perhaps, and obsessive—but what scientist isn't?

RRS: How did he treat his employees?

IB: With courtesy and respect. He was one of the politest, most well-mannered men I've ever known in my entire life.

4. Heart-shaped / Centrifugal Force

The situation deteriorated over time, in some respects. As the relationships among the three friends fell apart, each woman's relationship with me grew stronger. And as each of their relationships with me grew stronger, the greater was my confusion about it. Mysteriously, our work environment became increasingly childish. If Mathilde and I worked longer than was strictly necessary on a given task, Patricia Julia and Isadore would become furious with Mathilde; out of revenge, they wouldn't speak to her for the rest of the day, and they'd punish me by treating me with cool disdain. If, during lunch, Isadore and I sat down together to chat, the other two would join forces to chastise us with their collective indifference. The same would happen with Mathilde and Isadore if I dared to walk Patricia Julia to her car and if she lingered in order to talk with me a while in the parking lot. There was no way to maintain harmony. I was always doing something that upset our precarious balance, and I couldn't remedy the problem because I couldn't imagine what the problem might be.

Over time, and despite everything, we came to know one another quite well. Better said: I came to know them quite well. Terrified they'd discover my secret, I had no choice but to maintain my distance. So great was their zeal for asking me personal questions, for finding reasons to be near me, for initiating, through all possible means, conversations that had nothing to do with work, that many times I began to suspect that they were plotting my destruction.

The most insistent of the three was, without a doubt, Mathilde. About a month into our professional coexistence, she took up the habit of arriving earlier than the others, waiting in her car until I arrived, and only then getting out. She'd bid me good morning and immediately relieve me of my briefcase, or whatever else I was holding.

"Give it to me," she'd say. "That's what I'm here for."

"That isn't necessary, Álvarez," I'd resist. "I can manage on my own."

"Oh!" she'd fume. "You just love to annoy me. Call me Mathilde!"

"Okay," I'd say, "Mathilde, I can manage on my own."

"Perhaps," she'd reply, feigning anger. "Now give it to me and stop arguing."

Et cetera.

I remember the last time she was in my office.

"Helllloooo," she said, poking her head in the door. Loyda, my secretary, never could restrain her.

"Miss," I said with theatrical seriousness. We never got tired of this game.

"I'm sorry, sir," interjected Loyda, too late. "I told her that. . . ."

"Thank you, Loyda," I said. "It's all right."

"Yes, sir," said Loyda, retreating, but not before directing an intense look of hatred at Mathilde. As soon as she'd closed the door, Mathilde stuck her tongue out at her.

"What is it?" I said, not getting up. Mathilde walked over and sat on the edge of my desk, to my right, as usual. She was wearing a sky blue mini-skirt. Once again I was visited by that terrible sensation of vertigo, as though a chloroform-soaked handkerchief had just been waved under my nose.

"Nothing," she said, crossing her firm, pink legs. The feeling of succumbing to a powerful narcotic intensified; it's possible that the lavender-scented lotion she used to moisturize her thighs was causing me to have an allergic reaction. "I left the

centrifuge separating cells for a primary culture. It will be finished in half an hour."

"Excellent," I said in a conclusive tone. But then, as though
trapped in an inescapable magnetic field, I couldn't remove my
eyes from hers, nor could she remove hers from mine. To make
matters worse, neither one of us said anything. It was as though
she wanted to wrest a confession from me. She examined my
expression with such intensity that her eyes burned my face. It
lasted only a few seconds, but to me, it seemed an eternity.

"And you?" she finally said, swinging her legs and looking
away from me.

"Me?" I said, and surprised myself wishing, inexplicably,
that she'd go, that she'd leave me alone. "As you can see."

"Busy," she said sadly. With genuine sadness, the sadness of
a little girl who asks for and doesn't receive the attention she
needs. But why had she gotten like this so suddenly? Why didn't
she go downstairs to talk with her colleagues, or help them? Certainly they would have a great deal to do.

"Paperwork, paperwork, and more paperwork," I said. "Here
in the office, it's what I must do."

"Hmmm," she mused. "Is that why you came to our lab, to
flee your paperwork?"

"In a manner of speaking," I laughed.

"In a manner of speaking," she repeated very seriously, lift-
ing her leg and grazing my elbow with the pointed heel of her
shoe. "In a manner of speaking, of course."

Then the magnetic field again and silence. This time, however, she took pity on me.

"Well," she said, sliding smoothly off the desk to her feet,
"I'm going. I'll leave you to finish your paperwork, paperwork,
and more paperwork."

"I'll see you down there," I said. She walked slowly to the
door, paused, waved goodbye, and left. I felt enormously relieved.
But then I noticed that there was something in the place she'd

been sitting: small, heart-shaped, wrapped in red foil. A chocolate.

I went out after her. Luckily she'd not yet crossed the threshold out of my office.

"Mathilde," I said. She turned.

"Yes?" she replied. Loyda stopped typing and looked at us curiously.

"You dropped this," I said, holding out the chocolate. First, her face turned livid and then it ignited in a blazing red. She looked at Loyda. Loyda returned the look, reprimanding her with a small smile of contempt.

"Oh!" said Mathilde, brusquely grabbing the chocolate from me. "How stupid of me! Thank you."

She hurried off. I could hear the rapid-fire echo of her heels in the hallway.

That was Mathilde: intelligent and responsible, but extremely absent-minded.

ALCHEMY

AND

PHOTOSYNTHESIS

There are no emotions without a self that produces and experiences them. And vice versa: without emotions, the self doesn't exist. The self, that presence conscious of itself, encysted in our bodies, has a dynamic existence, constantly defined and redefined by the emotions it uses to interpret stimuli received by the senses. They are not separable entities.

To "be one's self" is our principal emotion.

Valérie's death caused me to lose this base stimulus and threw my life into total confusion. I finished school on autopilot, doing the impossible so as not to think. Nothing mattered to me. I felt nothing. I had ceased to "be myself." The loss, however, was not total; I could perceive, very vaguely, the need to recuperate that which had fled, not to remain forever with my arms crossed. For the time being though, I ignored the call almost completely.

I chucked the idea of preparing for entrance exams and getting back on the road to finish what was still required of me to become a doctor. I loathed the idea of investing the next two or three years reviewing material in order to obtain my license. I was horrified at the thought of then joining the mad rush of hundreds of my peers who kill themselves trying to conquer one of the only two or three vacant positions in a prestigious hospital. I wanted to get away from everything and everyone. I applied to graduate school at various universities in the United States. I was accepted to almost all of them. I chose one at random and left.

Those were years of profound meditation, of intense searching for answers. I attended classes that were not part of my curriculum: psychology, cognitive neurology, behavioral sciences. In under two semesters I understood in depth the insanity that had taken possession of Simònides. The trigger, however, remained a mystery to me. On one of my sporadic visits home I tried to talk to him. He'd never registered my presence in his house, had never spoken a word to me, and had no idea what my name was. He had surely thought that I was a domestic servant, a new one every time. To him we were all the same. I thought I could face him, but when I saw them bringing him in, and *how* they were bringing him in, I fled. I didn't see him again.

I made only two new friends at the university, both island girls like me, who made exile more bearable and who would become lifelong companions. But not even their unconditional friendship could rein in my obsession.

Intuiting that my educational panorama was expanding in an asymmetrical way, I ventured into the Humanities Department and registered for classes in sociology of religion, social anthropology, archeology, medical ethics. I joined student associations, political organizations, and volunteer aid groups in which I learned from my compatriots new and marvelous things about my parents' country, including, very *sotto voce*, interesting facts and anecdotes about the most famous and macabre of our exports. I never told the story about Adeline's business venture to anyone, and no one ever told me anything like it, either. I became a fan. I learned everything I could, and then I devoured, fascinated, the various Hollywood misrepresentations.

In the second to last semester of my program (towards which, despite my interdisciplinary adventures, I had more than adequate credits), I enrolled in a course on ethnobotany in which, miraculously, everything I'd learned during those years took shape and linked up together, revealing to me the perfection of a design from time immemorial in which everything and everyone is composed of the same substance. The world, in truth, is a manipulable structure. Each and every thing holds the possibility of becoming a master key capable of rewriting the rules of Nature. . . . Nothing realizes this possibility more powerfully and with more versatility than plants.

I wrote a thesis proposal. I applied for research grants and was awarded them. On the airplane I had time to reflect, and I realized that during the past few years, more than academic honors, more than a thirst for objective knowledge, I'd been impelled by a desire to find myself. I finally understood the carved inscription of the Delphic oracle. I possessed the secret, but I couldn't access it except through the meanderings of a journey of initiation that, stupidly, I'd believed I could undertake by seeking a doctorate in a university far from home. I needed to return and confront my origins.

Alchemists recorded the movements of the human spirit and its eventual transformation (the philosopher's stone) by observing the properties of the elements and their different combinations—revealing, at the same time, the secret composition of the world. I would do the same with the plants that those who still know how to speak the language of the earth use to repair the body, unleash the mind, and open or close the doors to the world.

That's what I'm doing here.

I've been camping out in the open countryside for three days, collecting specimens and moving slowly toward my grandparents' village, where, according to my father (roundly opposed to my expedition), a first cousin of his whom I've never met still lives.

5. Beast / A Natural Talent

Similar things happened to me with the others as well. One afternoon, as was her habit, Patricia Julia accompanied me to the parking lot, chatting ceaselessly. The soft, warm, six o'clock breeze rustled through her straight hair and lifted her skirt, revealing perfectly toned thighs.

". . . and that's why I'll never go back to La Tortuga," she said, finishing her long story. "I don't care how much the cosmos cost; they could sell them for a buck for all I care. Until they replace the felt on that billiards table, they can count me out. I'm boycotting. That's just how I am."

I nodded and smiled. There were never uncomfortable silences with Patricia Julia; she made it her business to talk for the both of us. We were almost to her car.

"The worst is that if I don't assert myself, Mathilde makes us go to some fancy lounge to listen to her tell the story about how her great-grandfather or great-great-grandfather discovered the tuberculosis bacillus. She drives us up the wall with the same old story."

"Doesn't Isadore ever suggest a place?"

"No. It's all the same to her."

She opened her car door, slid in behind the wheel, and looked me in the eye.

"Oh!" she exclaimed, suddenly remembering something. "Come, sit here, I want to show you some photos."

I obeyed. I circled around the car and got in next to her. She opened her computer and set it on my lap, first making sure that no one else was prowling about the parking lot.

"They're from last weekend," she said, indicating the slide

show. The first image was of the three friends in bathing suits, arm in arm. Patricia Julia was in the middle; the blue sea behind. The sand was a dazzling white. They looked like happy nymphs. The next photo was of the friends sunning themselves on wicker mats. Blinding glints of sunlight reflected off the lenses of their sunglasses. Their bodies were so perfect, their poses so natural, the photo looked like a postcard or a beer advertisement. The next were photos of Patricia Julia and Mathilde playing in the water; Patricia Julia posing with a surfboard; Mathilde and Isadore, their hair wet, sitting at the bar of some beach dive drinking daiquiris; all three under a palm tree, drying off with brightly colored towels. Patricia Julia couldn't see very well from her seat, so she leaned in near me and rested her head on my shoulder. I felt like a hand made of feathers was rooting about in my stomach.

The rest of the photos were of Patricia Julia in her bikini: from the back, looking coquettishly at the camera and tipping up her smooth, nearly naked buttocks; sitting on the sand with her knees bent, leaning back on her hands; from the side, resting her arms on the bar, one leg propped up on the rung of a stool, the other on the ground, the roundness of her rear accentuated by the tautness of her tiny waist—and suddenly, Patricia Julia in what appeared to be her bedroom, a dreamy expression on her face, leaning against a chest of drawers, one leg on the bed, her right hand untying the strings of her bikini bottom. I could feel Patricia Julia's breath at my side, very close, a subtle and ardent panting. Her nearness, and the fact that the inside of the car amplified the silence, alerted me to the possibility that she'd realize that only she inhaled and exhaled air through the lungs. The last photo showed her in bed, her naked body carelessly wrapped in a silk throw. The feathery hand fumbling about in my stomach began to close around my throat, strangling me. At that moment, Patricia Julia closed the computer with a slow and deliberate motion.

"What did you think of them?" she asked without moving her head from its position on my shoulder.

"They're very nice," I said, turning my head to look at her. I was surprised to find the same expression from the last photo on her face, a languid look of absolute docility and surrender.

"And?" she asked. I did the only thing I was capable of: I told her the truth.

"I think you have a natural talent."

Patricia Julia rested her chin on my shoulder and looked at me, perplexed. I could see that she was not satisfied, so I elaborated.

"Well . . . I don't know. Perhaps you went to modeling school. I don't remember reading that part of your résumé but the truth is you're an extraordinary model, almost a professional. All of the photos are lovely, but yours are exceptional. Technically, the photos leave much to be desired, but this could well be due to deficiencies of the digital camera. It has nothing to do with you, you're not a photographer. The important thing is that any bathing suit or lingerie designer would sign you in a heartbeat. . . ."

Patricia Julia pulled away from me and fixed me with her gaze. Her mouth made a grimace of disbelief; she must have thought I was pulling her leg. I reassured her.

"Seriously!" I exclaimed. Her only reply was to take the computer from my lap and set it on the backseat, put up her hair, and start the car.

"See you tomorrow," she said, as she adjusted the rear view mirror, preparing to back up.

"Of course," I said, getting out. "See you tomorrow."

I closed the door and she accelerated immediately, without taking the proper precautions. Luckily, I'd already grown accustomed to her unpredictable behavior and her inexplicable reactions.

THE THREE STAGES OF VINDICATION

My command of Creole leaves much to be desired. Due to my ineptitude, the following narrative has lost the regional peculiarities and subtle shades of meaning of the manner of speech of my second cousin, Sandrine Bellamy. I'm no translator. I've rendered her story in words and phrases that are familiar to me; I was not tempted by rigorous accuracy. I warn you, however, that the apparent refinement of her narrative does not come from me. Sandrine is village head, a rank occupied only by those who display, from childhood, oratorical skills, great erudition, and a rich command of the lexicon. They are the village's memory.

City people make fun of us. They make fun of our ignorance. It's fair. We make merciless fun of the city dwellers that pass through here every now and again. These occasional visitors belong to one of two types: those who come to our village accidentally, and those who don't. The first are lost tourists, thirsty state topographers, speculators full of incomprehensible questions, drug traffickers scouting new contraband routes. The rest are Salesian missionaries, evangelical preachers, functionaries from some international aid organization or another, anthropologists, people who come to understand and save us. . . . But there's nothing to understand and no one to save, except themselves. None ever lasts more than one night with us, maybe two, and it's all because of our brothers and sisters from the neighboring village, at the foot of the valley, where the cashew trees grow.

There, in the city, we're ridiculous. It's fun to see a simple servant girl open canned goods with a knife and a rock, and more fun still to see her expression, one of total vacuity, when they tell her to use a can opener. "A what?" I know this well.

I don't blame them. It makes us laugh to see a casual visitor sit down underneath a wasps' nest that he's too stupid to detect, drink water from the lagoons downriver where our waste accumulates, or struggle with horses and mules that disobey him unequivocally, grazing away in utter tranquility.

It was the same with your father; it didn't matter a bit that we were cousins. The logical direction was from the countryside to the city, so whenever the opportunity arose (summer vacations, floods, plagues), I was the one to make the long journey to my aunt and uncle's house. The idea, I suppose, was that on one of those trips my return would be somehow thwarted, and I'd stay there. The less time in the countryside, the better. But my aunt and uncle always sent me back, not before first taking advantage of my stay to press me into servants' duties. This practice also obeyed an irrefutable logic. The poor relative had to justify her presence, make herself useful. Your grandfather, my uncle, was very decent and affectionate towards me, but he spent the entire day at his grocery and had no idea what went on in the house. Your grandmother, my aunt-in-law, was another story. She wasn't born here, she was from over there, and she never missed the opportunity to point out the difference between us by treating me like an animal or a slave; I washed clothes, hung them out to dry, tidied the bedrooms, cooked, swept, scrubbed, took out the trash. And when I had finally finished my chores, when she couldn't think of anything else for me to do and I was happy because I was going to be able to go out and play with my cousins and friends, she'd invent absurd errands for me or insist upon the existence of imaginary dirt and stains on the floors, walls, dishes, and clothes that I had just finished washing. I was made to keep working until night fell and we all had to go to bed.

She didn't allow me to watch television, except when she had

her friends from the neighborhood or relatives over, because then
she'd make jokes at my expense, making them believe that I was
convinced that the people who appeared on the screen could see
us as clearly as we could see them. I confess that I did think that
the first time I saw the contraption, exciting the ridicule of the
entire household, but this error of perception did not last more
than an instant. From then on my Madam Aunt would reconstruct for her audience, with me sitting in front of the television,
every detail of my stupidity. Her enthusiasm for the story made
me suspect that the same thing had happened to her when she'd
had her first encounter with the invention—and that it hadn't
exactly been when she was a child, either. On the other hand, the
smugness and arrogance of her guests' mockery led me to understand that the intensity of their guffaws was directly proportional
to the vehemence of their wish to forget the fact that they'd made
it all the way through adolescence and, in some cases, even into
adulthood, wiping their asses with corncobs. Ex-peasants, or the
children of ex-peasants, splashing about on the outskirts of the
city but behaving in front of their rustic relatives as though they
lived in the magical city of a children's fairy tale.

This is why I was so elated when my uncle sent word to my
father that Pascal would be spending that summer with us. He
had, apparently, caused some sort of scandal at school, a brawl,
on top of which he brought home a disastrous report card. They
were sending him to us as punishment. Except for me, no one in
my family knew enough to detect the implicit insult: to live with
us for any amount of time was a humiliation. I imagine that the
logic I mentioned before prevailed. In that direction, civilization, wealth, prosperity, the future. In this direction, the past,
the jungle, insects, agony. Here, we must screw our faces up
against the elements; it is impossible to forget that you live in
the world, and the world prevents you from forgetting its shape
and its dangers. There, one rests one's head upon a lie of asphalt
and concrete that pretends to be a substitute for the world and

that rewards those who allow themselves to be fooled with a rich assortment of misery and violence and selfishness.

Your grandfather's instructions to his younger brother, my father, were very clear: Pascal should be put to work doing all types of country tasks without special consideration. It's true that if we hadn't had those instructions Pascal wouldn't have done anything except sleep and get fat. Those of us who live here greatly pity the weakness and ignorance of those who live over there; we make accommodations for them, we spoil them; they are, for us, helpless creatures. But we wouldn't do this with Pascal. Especially not me. The moment for my revenge had arrived.

I had planned everything out coldly and methodically. You could tell I was excited, I was dying of anticipation, and my mother thought that I must be smitten with my cousin. My revenge would unfold in various stages, three in particular:

1. *Family Disgrace.* I would remember all the times Pascal had allied with his mother and seconded her torments and celebrated her jokes in front of the rest of our cousins and other relatives both near and distant, and I would make him pay for them one by one. I wouldn't have to strain my memory much. How could I forget, for example, the time that he walked into the living room full of people, belly-laughing and waving like a flag the underpants I'd hung out to dry in the backyard, streaked with the pink shadow of an unexpected period, and shouting that I wore old ladies' underwear?

2. *Public Infamy.* The few times I was allowed to go out to play in the neighborhood streets or at the park, Pascal rejected me in front of his friends and denied that he understood what I was telling him in Creole. He would mimic me in a singsong jeer, in a savage key, making discordant sounds and waving his arms, making it known that I was some sort of cannibal. In order to avoid this I began using what little Spanish I knew back then, but that only made it worse.

3. *Physical Ruin.* I never worked as hard in my village as I did at my aunt and uncle's house. Pascal never did anything, ever. This was to be his first experience in the world of physical labor. And here, the men are required to do the most onerous tasks. I myself would take charge of multiplying and making them more unpleasant than necessary for him.

My cousin finally arrived one Saturday at lunchtime. We hadn't yet finished eating when it already became clear that my plans would fail miserably.

6. Intellectual / Wicked Weeds

It was the same with Isadore—but different. She also sought me out and did everything possible to overshadow the others. Her stratagems, however, were of a more discreet and sophisticated character. Introverted by nature, Isadore preferred to observe how her friends progressed with me and to be present every time our interactions activated some mysterious explosion that caused them to become angry for no reason. Isadore was haughty, proud, and overly intelligent. She never put herself in disadvantageous positions, which is to say that she avoided creating circumstances consonant with my apparent inability to keep them happy. For this reason I got along better with her than with the others; I felt comfortable and I didn't worry so much about offending her by accident. For this reason I allowed her, once, to take me home with her.

It was raining. Rain is a zombie's worst enemy; anyone could imagine why. I took advantage of a lull to try to get to my car and leave before it intensified again, but when I got there I saw that one of my tires was completely flat. I crouched down to inspect it; it had been lanced with a precise cut. A vandal. At that moment Isadore pulled up in her car alongside me, rolled down the window, and regarded the tire.

"Come on," she said. "I live nearby. We'll call the insurance company from my house and arrange for them to send their people out to put on a replacement. I'll bring you back when it's ready."

"Don't trouble yourself, Doctor," I replied. "I'll go back to the office and call from there."

The damp air gradually filled again with fat raindrops and

the wind began to pick up with the promise of a torrential storm.

"As you wish," said Isadore just then, allowing her car to advance slowly.

"On second thought," I said, taking a step forward.

"Get in," said Isadore, stopping again. Before leaving, we informed the afternoon guard of what had happened.

"Forgive me," he said. "It's strange. No one has come in here without authorization. The only people in the par . . ."

"It doesn't matter," interrupted Isadore. "Whatever happened, happened. Now I'd like you to wait for the repair truck the insurance company is going to send out."

"Yes, Doctor."

"Here," I said, handing him the keys to my car.

"My shift is over, but I'll let the next guy know before I leave."

"Perfect."

Isadore lived four blocks away, on the fourteenth floor of an elegant condominium building.

"I bought the apartment at half price," she told me as we rode up the elevator, pointing to the numbers lighting up successively. "Look closely and then guess why."

Nine, ten, eleven, twelve, . . . fourteen? There was no thirteenth floor, numerically speaking.

"A mathematical miracle," I said.

"Fourteen is the thirteenth floor," said Isadore. The elevator doors opened and we emerged into a dim hallway. "People think that if they don't see the number that the numerical concept that follows twelve and precedes fourteen ceases to exist."

"It seems like few fall for the trick. Otherwise, they wouldn't sell it so cheaply."

"That's right," said Isadore, turning her keys and unlocking the door. "What do you think of the twenty-first century? . . . Come in."

The apartment was spacious, decorated with exquisite taste. There were books everywhere, not only on the many bookshelves, but also on the windowsills, the floor, the dining room table, the top of the kitchen cabinets. In the canvasses hung on the walls I recognized the unmistakable strokes of Richard Santiago, Rafael Trelles, José García Cordero, Eleomar Puente—originals, worth a small fortune. On small end tables I saw African fetishes, statues of the Buddha, teak incense burners. Some of the armchairs were decorated with beautiful Hindu tapestries, Panamanian *molas*, and Haitian *vévés*. Isadore indicated a chair.

"Make yourself at home," she said, and disappeared into the interior of the apartment. I was alone in the dimly lit living room, and suddenly time seemed to stretch like a rubber band, getting longer and thinner and also tenser, more energized. When Isadore reappeared it was as though the rubber band returned to its natural shape with a violent snap.

"Here you are," she said, handing me a cordless phone. I suddenly remembered the reason for my presence in her home. I took out my billfold and pulled out my insurance card. While I made the pertinent calls, Isadore went to work in the kitchen.

"I'm making you a drink," she said without asking me what I wanted to drink or if I wanted anything to drink at all. I was familiar with her talent for being domineering; it was her greatest managerial quality.

"Thank you," I said in a resigned tone of voice. I was feeling slightly dizzy, but it wasn't that exactly. It was a kind of general relaxation. I didn't want to think about anything. The only thing I wanted was to stay stretched out in the chair Isadore had offered me, in the shadows, waiting for my drink. In peace.

Isadore approached me with a glass just as I was finishing with my insurance agent about the repair of my vehicle. It was a skillfully concocted bloody mary, served in the proper glass and even garnished with a celery stalk—a drink prepared by someone who has followed the recipe to the letter.

"Thank you," I said, suddenly and inexplicably uncomfortable.

"Stop thanking me," she said, and then I understood the reason for my discomfort: I had also realized, without realizing it, that I was repeating myself like a nincompoop. "You sound like a broken record."

We laughed. We drank, in unison, a sip of the tomato concoction.

"What do you think?" she asked.

"Mmmm . . . ," I said. Isadore smiled.

"There's no higher compliment," she said, sitting on the sofa across from me, "than the moans that issue from the soul."

"Pardon?" I said, having no idea what she was talking about. And to make matters worse, I don't even have a soul. Hoping to avoid a misunderstanding, I reiterated: "It's delicious." A confused expression swept across her face like a gust of wind, but, a fraction of a second later, she gave me another white smile. She rescued a small remote from a nearby table and pressed a button. Seconds later, Emeline Michel's delicious voice, issuing from speakers whose location I couldn't establish, took possession of the inviting room.

"Do you like my house?" she asked.

"I love it," I said.

"That's better. Why do you love it?"

I couldn't respond. Isadore was looking at me with a glimmer of malice. I couldn't find the words to answer her logically, not because I was nervous but because I didn't understand what she was asking me.

"It's beautiful," I insisted.

"Thank you," she said, continuing to fix me with those flashing eyes. I noticed that she was delighting in my failure; she drank from her glass. "If I were naughty, now I'd ask you *why* it's beautiful."

I surprised myself mentally begging that she wouldn't.

"I *am* naughty," she said, setting her glass on a table, enjoying herself. "But I won't do it."

I let out an involuntary sigh. I'm quite skilled at faking these types of vital signs when the circumstances require it; I don't know why it came so naturally this time, without my even meaning to, especially when the most rational thing would be to hide my relief from her.

I needed to change the subject immediately. Near me there was a shelf containing movies on DVD. I took advantage of the opportunity, not suspecting that I was diving headlong into a bottomless pit.

"I see that you like movies," I said.

"I collect zombie films," she said. Only then did it occur to me to read the titles. I had to get out of there. But how to do it without arousing suspicion?

"Really?" I said.

"Yes," said Isadore, winking at me. "I love them."

"I never would have guessed," I said, swallowing a nonexistent mouthful of saliva. How bothersome this sudden and involuntary mania for imitating conventional bodily processes! All I needed now was to raise my hand to my heart as though I were suffering from tachycardia.

"Well, yes," said Isadore cheerfully. "Take a look, check if you've seen any of them."

I, of course, had seen *all* of them. Her collection was quite comprehensive. I decided that the best way to avoid Isadore's discovering or suspecting the truth was to be enthusiastic.

"I do know a few," I said, feigning interest.

"Do tell!" she said, widening her eyes with disbelief.

"Enough to know that you've organized your collection

chronologically," I said, "and that, between *I Walked with a Zombie*, from 1943, and *Zombies of Mora Tau*, of 1957, you're missing *Zombies on Broadway*, from 1944. Unless you've loaned it out."

"Ah!" exclaimed Isadore. "I'm in the presence of a connoisseur."

"No, no," I said, with false humility, "not at all, not at all."

"The premise is quite original, quite funny," said Isadore. "The owner of a night club wants to use a zombie in his act—but a real zombie. You could say it's a story along the lines of *King Kong* and *Mighty Joe Young*."

"Both by Ernst Schoedsack," I said. "Shall we ascribe it to the ethos of a historical period, or to the traumas of specific individuals?"

"It doesn't matter," replied Isadore. "The unsettling part is the insistence of the supernatural as phenomenon, the phenomenon as blockbuster. They're self-referential narratives. A spectacle about a spectacle. What I never liked about *Zombies on Broadway* was the physical humor. I detest slapstick. Bela Lugosi didn't deserve that indignity."

"And yet," I commented, "I see that you have *Plan 9 from Outer Space*. . . ."

"It's not the same thing," she said. "I'm not saying it isn't kitsch, which it is, but there's no clowning about."

She was right. And anyway, no zombie movie collection could ever be complete without that masterpiece by Ed Wood. The holy trinity of horror, Bela Lugosi, Tor Johnson, and Vampira portray zombies controlled by sinister aliens carrying out a master plan (the ninth plan) to dominate planet Earth.

"And what do you have to say about this one," I asked, holding up *The Incredibly Strange Creatures Who Stopped Living and Became Crazy Mixed-Up Zombies*, a B movie from 1964. Isadore burst out laughing.

"Guilty as charged," she said.

Not that they ever come out very well, but, under the circumstances I had to do it, so I plagiarized a guffaw. It was a stupid move. The coarse wheeze of a broken accordion punctuated by asthmatic hisses and a fit of indigestion horrified Isadore, who was now looking at me in consternation. I coughed to distract her and to offer some plausible explanation for roaring like a psychopath with a cold. Only then did she start smiling again.

With the exception of the Japanese parody *Biozombie*, none of the rest of the movies in her collection inspired humor. We're talking about the classics of the genre, from its infancy (*Invasion of the Zombies, I Eat Your Skin, Carnival of Souls*) through to its latest period (*Dead Alive, Cemetery Man, Army of Darkness, Junk*). With dizzying lucidity, Isadore considered the George A. Romero trilogy, thoughtfully weighing the political, racial, and sexual aspects converging in the plots. For Romero, according to Isadore, chaos, and the rapid disintegration of the social apparatus brought about by the appearance of the living dead, is a metaphor for the tensions implicit in a system of multicultural coexistence and the artistic representation par excellence of the anguished, paranoid, white middle class in the United States.

"Or," I interjected, "it's simply an attempt to subvert the Judeo-Christian concept of the resurrection of the flesh, twisting it sufficiently to take it to its ultimate consequences. A sublime way of asserting that Judgment Day will take the form of an ecological cataclysm."

"It could be," she agreed. "It could be because, think about it, the horror of these films, especially those from the North American school, depends less on the hideousness of the zombie than on the *quantity* of zombies."

"The number is the monster, correct. A single zombie isn't scary."

"And not just any number, but a number that grows exponentially."

"The terror of being overcome and transformed by hordes of

irrational and foul-smelling beings, a fright as American as apple pie."

"As opposed to Lucio Fulci's films," put in Isadore happily, "in which everything depends on the makeup, the special effects, and the exaggeratedly repulsive scenes."

"One can always count on Italy for that."

She laughed. I suppressed the desire to imitate her. I coughed, because I'm good at that, and, when all is said and done, it's a spasm of the thorax not all that different from laughter.

Our conversation went on for more than an hour. It was all I could do to keep up with her. In my first years as a zombie I forced myself to study the blood-curdling representations of our terrible condition in popular culture and mass media. It was my way of cultivating a necessary discomfort with my surroundings. I knew that I must never allow myself to be lulled into a false sense of security. There were dangers at every turn. For the living we are nothing more than a gruesome and diabolical source of contagion. It seemed absurd to me, that scandalous misrepresentation of the process by which one becomes a zombie—how the entire ritual of it is precluded, the numinous aspects of it and, especially, the pharmacological complexity of the zombie dust. The film industry simplifies everything, resorting to a viral interpretation, as though it were rabies, mononucleosis, or hepatitis B. I quickly became an expert in order to survive. What was Isadore's excuse?

In addition to the films, Isadore had collected early novels and stories in which the zombie becomes an icon of modern horror: treasures such as *Salt Is Not for Slaves*, by G. W. Hutter; *The House in the Magnolias*, by August Derleth; and William Seabrook's infamous account, *The Magic Island*. Isadore even showed me a story from 1926, *Jumbee*, written by a certain Henry S. Whitehead, based on his experiences as an archdeacon in the Virgin Islands.

"Jumbee?" I asked.

"Jumbee, zombie," she said. "It's the same word, pronounced differently, and it means more or less the same thing. The jumbee of the Lesser Antilles is a relatively incorporeal being, while the zombie we know carries his decay on his back."

Isadore explained to me that the oldest reference to zombies is found in a novel from 1697, *Le Zombi du Grand-Perou ou la Contesse de Cocagne*, written by Paul-Alexis Blessepois. This was a fact I hadn't known, and I asked her to show me the book. She promised to make a high-quality photocopy of it for me first thing the next morning.

That night I discovered that Isadore was also an expert on Caribbean pharmacopeia. With the cautious vivacity of a pre-teen, she showed me the voluminous field journal that she had compiled for a research project she'd done once upon a time, back when she was a graduate student doing a subspecialty in ethnobotany.

Isadore was proud of her work. She turned the pages of her journal with extreme care so as not to wrinkle them. My eyes followed the parsimonious movements of her black hands with the same automatic rapture of a moth around a flame. Exquisitely rendered in charcoal, Isadore's sketches detailed the slightly coriaceous valves of the *tcha-tcha* pod, properly identified as *Albizia lebbeck*. Further on were the imparipinnate leaves of the *Trichilia hirta*, better known on the islands as *matapiojo* or *conejo colorado*; the dangerous and urticant white trichomes of the *Mucuna pruriens*; the pungent hairs of the *Urera baccifera*; the sharply pointed leaves of the abominable *Comocladia glabra*; and many other plants that make up our colorful and poisonous tropical *guasábara*.

Each entry was comprised of a sketch, notes, and sometimes a small Polaroid that showed, or didn't, Isadore in shorts, squatting next to the plant, or only her hands manipulating the stems, or her standing in the shade of a thicket. There were images and snippets that suggested other scenarios: a small village with cobblestone streets; a group of barefoot children making faces and waving and piling on top of one another in order to be in the photo; Isadore hugging an older woman with the same oblique eyes as hers; a field sown with yellow and red cashew trees. The text that accompanied the visual material did not necessarily correspond to the images shown. Many of the entries, which I read as quickly as I could before Isadore turned the page, had nothing to do with the drawings of the plants or the photos encircled in her meticulous cursive. Some were brief disquisitions on neurobiological themes, ideas written down in a rush to be elaborated on later; others were transcriptions of stories or of conversations that she'd collected during her expedition. She'd wanted to preserve all of it. It was an intricate and chaotic scrapbook that did not obey the dictates of any sort of linear progression. It was obvious that Isadore had created it on the go, opening it at random and using the first blank page her eye fell upon. Clearly, Isadore was a slave to the right hemisphere of her brain. Of course, this is the sort of thing that only those of us who are slaves to the left side would notice. But what zombie isn't?

Isadore would pause at a recorded specimen, detailing its properties for me, believing that she was opening the doors to a marvelous world, wanting to share with me the emotion of making a discovery out in the field, outfitted with a compass and water canteens, far away from any city. But I couldn't accompany her on that nostalgic journey, or at least not in the way she wanted me to. I couldn't because I already knew those plants all too well. Because I'm dead and my blood vessels collapsed some time ago, I didn't get goosebumps, a phenomenon caused by the sudden constriction of the epidural capillaries. Nevertheless, I felt the echo of that old sensation, growing stronger by the minute, as Isadore turned the pages . . . because all of the plants in her journal, every single one of them, were fundamental ingredients of zombie dust.

"This one, for example," said Isadore, showing me an unmistakable drawing of the wild radish, also called mother-in-law's tongue, "the *Dieffenbachia seguine*, contains calcium oxalate crystals in its leaves. These crystals irritate cell tissues and cause inflammation. Even so, it's quite popular as a decorative indoor plant."

Quite so, I thought. In fact, the plants in her catalog could be divided into two general groups: anesthetics and urticants. Zombie dust is a topical preparation, such that without the latter the drug would never succeed in contaminating the bloodstream. The damage caused, ironically, is self-inflicted: the intense itching they produce causes the victim to violently scratch himself, facilitating the penetration of the active components.

I didn't know what to think; I was finding it difficult to put my thoughts in order. One part of me persisted in wanting to defend the secret of my true nature, but at the same time I could feel an indescribable longing to confide in her growing within me. Who was Isadore? A possible ally or an undercover enemy? I had before me a true specialist in one of the cardinal lines of my own research. Isadore would, without a doubt, be extremely useful to me, but what had motivated her to study these plants in particular? What was she hiding? Was her interest authentic, or did she belong, perhaps, to one of those antizombie groups that pop up all over the place, organized by upright citizens—or worse, to a secret governmental office dedicated to the eradication of the living dead? I needed to determine what her work with these plants was really all about, find out if she could help me get my research back on track, ask her, perhaps, for her active collaboration. But how to do this without raising suspicions? I needed to make a quick decision. I opted for ambiguity.

"The plants in your herbarium all have something in common," I said, to see if she'd take the bait. I regretted it almost immediately. She did not raise her eyes from her journal to reply. I knew instantly that I'd fallen into my own trap.

"Really?" she said. "What would that be?"

I'd tried to force her to confess and the trick came right back to me like a boomerang. How could I have been so stupid? Why had it not occurred to me to say the same thing in the form of a question? Now I'd be forced to give the answer—or perhaps not? I risked it.

"I don't know," I said. "I'm asking you."

She started laughing, as though she had understood my dilemma and my manner of resolving it had struck her as funny. She took a lock of hair between her fingers and began to twirl it.

"One or two have medicinal uses, according to some sources," she said, shrugging her shoulders. "But, in reality, almost all of them sting. No one wants them in their gardens. They're plants that people pull out. Is that what you meant?"

"Of course, of course," I said, accepting defeat. "That's what I meant."

But then, I couldn't contain myself.

"It's odd, nonetheless," I insisted.

"What do you find odd?" she said, closing the journal.

"That someone would invest so much time studying and cataloging useless plants."

Isadore looked at me resentfully; she put the journal away on its shelf and let out a loud sigh, as would one who'd grown bored.

"Oh, I don't know," she said, standing up and moving away from me. "Perhaps I have a special predilection for wicked weeds."

She went to the kitchen, grabbed her key ring, and jingled it in her hand.

"Your car must be ready by now, don't you think?"

I had completely forgotten about my car. If, moments before, you'd asked me what I was doing in Isadore's house, I wouldn't have known how to answer. Now, everything was coming back to me: the downpour, the flat tire, Isadore, the insurance company. . . . All of that seemed to have happened centuries ago, the memory of a primordial era.

We made the return trip in silence. Isadore seemed irritated. Why? I don't know. It had stopped raining, but the traffic was still moving slowly, timidly—the exaggerated caution of prudish drivers on wet streets. It was already dark night by the time we arrived at the parking lot.

The repair truck was there. The mechanic was chatting animatedly with the night guard, the zombie who'd tried to become friendly with me at first when I used to arrive at work early in the morning. Recently I'd learned that the poor devil's shift began at dusk and stretched until the wee hours of the morning. I couldn't ignore him now; surely he'd helped the mechanic.

"Make sure everything's in order," Isadore told me. "I'll wait."

I got out. It was gloomy. I don't know how to explain it, but even before I got close to them I knew that the mechanic was a zombie too. He'd exchanged a furtive glance with the guard, some gesture of understanding passing between them as they saw me walking toward them, imperceptible to anyone else but not to me. The empty deference with which he greeted me confirmed my suspicion.

"Good evening," I said dryly.

"Doctor," said the guard.

"Sir," said the mechanic, removing his hat like a page. Imbecile. In our interactions, generally speaking, zombies vacillate between extremes of arrogant brazenness and overfamiliarity and the most slavish abjection. Experience had taught me that the intensity of this bad habit was inversely proportional to the zombie's level of education. They either unilaterally impose an insufferable lassitude in their social interactions, in the name of our common affliction, or they prostrate themselves like beggars, employing doleful courtesies.

"Don't do that, you idiot," said the guard to the mechanic. "Can't you see that you're annoying the doctor? Forgive him, please. He has manners from a different era. This good fellow is old-fashioned . . ."

"I have no idea what you're taking about," I objected. The shrewdness and obvious sarcasm of his words disconcerted me.

"Of course not," replied the guard with an ironic and somewhat arrogant expression.

"I beg your forgiveness, Sir," said the mechanic.

"There's nothing to forgive," I said. "Is my car ready?"

"The doctor is an important person, Calisto," put in the guard. "His time is very valuable. Don't imagine that he'll strike up a conversation with you. How could you even think that a person such as he would lower himself to talk with someone like you? Have a bit of consideration, my friend, and let the good doctor go, he must be tired and wanting to get home to his luxurious residence after an arduous day at work."

"A thou . . . thousand apologies, Sir," stammered the mechanic. "I didn't mean to. . . ."

"Does it amuse you to make fun of me?" I asked the guard. "Is that it?"

"What?" he said, aghast. "Whatever gave you that idea?"

"Here is your key, Sir," said the mechanic, showing me the keychain in the palm of his hand, moving away from the guard, his distance leading me to understand that he was not participating in the other's insolence. "Please, I just need your signature here."

I signed the proffered receipts. The guard never took his eyes off me.

"Hn!" he exclaimed, looking skyward. "Another storm is brewing. You'd better hurry, Doctor. It looks like it's going to start raining again, and you don't like to get wet. You might catch a cold—or something worse."

"What is your problem?" I demanded.

"The elements are unforgiving to those of us with weak constitutions," he said, ignoring me. "Fortunately, you enjoy a position that allows you to send others into the wind and weather while you take shelter with your young *pití* in some cozy corner."

It had been a long time since I'd heard that term of address, coined by resentful and belligerent hicks. The guard's audacity was escalating. I looked back furtively to be sure that Isadore was still waiting in her car. I wouldn't have wanted her to overhear anything that was passing between us. I took a step forward and confronted the guard. The mechanic, by now truly shocked, stepped between us.

"Sir! Sir!" he said, leading me quickly to my car. The guard looked at me impassively. The mechanic opened the trunk to show me where he had put the damaged tire. "Look. I put it in here. I don't think you'll be able to repair it. You'll have to buy another one. Look here: do you see? The cut is too long. It can't be sealed up, especially not from this side. Someone did this, a wrongdoer, Sir, with a very large knife. Do you see?"

So it was. The guard came over to look.

"Well now," he said. "What a pity! Such terrible times we live in. Such times! Where will it end? One can't even leave his car in the guarded parking lot of a huge company. The criminals know no limits, respect nothing."

I closed the trunk purposefully. The mechanic stepped to one side, his eyes on the ground. I started walking toward Isadore.

"And *your* car specifically," continued the guard, raising his voice. "That's the strangest part. And here I'd thought that you were beloved and respected by all. How wrong I was!"

I opened the door and sat down next to Isadore.

"Well?" she said. "Is everything okay?"

"Looks like it," I said. "Thank you for everything. I won't keep you any longer. See you tomorrow."

"See you tomorrow," she replied. "If there's anything else I can do for you, give me a call. Okay? You have my number."

"No," I said. "Actually . . ."

"Give me just a sec," said Isadore, and she leaned across me to open the glove compartment: a mini-flashlight, papers, envelopes, pens of various colors, a comb, bank deposit slips. . . .

"Hold this for me, please," she said, dropping all of that miscellany on my lap: a burned-out light bulb, a compass, a pencil without a point, a fluorescent rosary, a puka anklet, a wad of napkins, and, last of all, an enormous and very sharp looking survival knife.

"Aha!" she burst out, plucking up a little white card, the very last thing remaining in the glove compartment. "Here. I don't understand how you don't have my number. How absentminded of you."

"Thank you," I said. "And now, go get some rest."

I put everything back in the glove compartment. I got out, closed the door, and waited until she'd gone. When I could no longer see her taillights, I turned and stepped forward. Now I felt good and ready to tell that odious guard a thing or two without worrying that Isadore would hear us. By his attitude and his cynical words I didn't doubt in the least that he himself had caused the damage. But now I couldn't see him anywhere. The mechanic had also gone. The next morning I'd lodge a formal complaint with the Office of Human Resources.

P–Zed

In lower-level organisms the senses report directly to the motor cortex. These centers dictate the corresponding actions. It is not necessary to pay the emotional toll.

The rat discovers the cat and flees, and although he behaves at all times like an animal invaded by the human emotion we call "fear," he doesn't feel it. The rat does not possess a *self* that values it. Nevertheless, it survives.

Corollary: The visible signs of an emotion do not constitute the emotion. It is possible to exhibit behaviors similar to those engendered by emotions without emotion ever intervening, in other words, without any "self" being present to validate them.

Corollary: The conscious self is not indispensable to survival.

We see them every single day: on the streets, in tatters, digging through garbage cans—or in the newspapers, crowned by success.

In order to reach either extreme it is necessary to dispossess oneself of the central emotional censor.

Both extremes are interchangeable.

7. Zombie Dreams / Chamber of Miracles

We zombies don't sleep, but something akin to sleep overcomes us: at the end of our daily activities, and in a relatively unpredictable way, we lose all notion of time. Our "awakening" is a sudden return to reality; we cannot account for what's happened in the previous four or five hours. So-called lost time. Clocks surprise us with improbable leaps; we blink and already it's dawn. Death has snatched from us all biological indicators, from the most important down to the most trivial, but for some as yet unknown reason we remain shackled to the circadian rhythm. Clearly, sleep is an activity that exceeds the purely organic.

The night when it all happened, Mathilde, Patricia Julia, and Isadore woke me from one of these trances. I had fallen "asleep" at my lab bench, collapsed atop my notes and chaotic formulas. My research into zombie powder had led me down a blind alley; I understood perfectly the chemical chain reactions that occurred in the body until achieving the effective suspension of biological activities. I understood, furthermore, the biochemical process which, at the end of a very precise period of time, reanimated the muscle tissues, reactivated the nervous system, and allowed for the continuation of consciousness. But I had not been able to discover why this resurrection was *not* accompanied by the reinstatement of *all* vital functions. The *appearance* of life stirred anew in the organism, but the organism itself remained on indefinite standby. The body's machinery did not start up again. My objective was to correct this gap: either to disband consciousness once and for all (and die completely) or to reinstate life to the body (and *live* in accordance with the dictionary definition—live like everyone else).

Although the majority of the components of zombie dust are of plant origin, the active ingredient is an animal by-product: the puffer fish toxin, known as tetrodotoxin. This poison is a simple substance that blocks the connectivity of axons, the neural nodes that transmit electrical impulses. As a consequence, the voluntary muscles are disabled. The toxin also affects the vascular system, dilating the vessels and thus causing a drop in arterial pressure. The functioning of the hypothalamus is also interrupted, causing a sudden drop in body temperature and hormonal unbalance. I am still not entirely certain how this happens, but I suspect that the toxic molecules seal off the neural sodium ion channels, disrupting the voltage of the nervous cells. Of course, in zombies this original voltage is never reestablished. We are ruined vessels, broken-down engines whose gears keep turning in the dark, on their own, with no metabolism, kindled by a dark force, impossible, nonenergetic. And therein lies the key. I know it. But I cannot visualize the solution in terms of molecular structure—it's as though I were overlooking something fundamental. But what?

I said earlier that we zombies sleep—in our own way. Some of us also dream. Our dreams, however, are not the least bit like the psycho-oneiric events to which the living are accustomed. When a living person dreams, he can sometimes be a participant in the dream and at other times simply a spectator. In zombie dreams the dreamer is *always* an eyewitness to the dream, never an actor in it. One might say that we don't really dream, but rather, that we *see* dreams.

On that crucial night I *saw* a dream. If only I could parse its meaning . . . I intuit that within the conjunction of symbols and convoluted metaphors hides the secret ingredient I'm lacking.

It began in the same way my zombie dreams always begin: I find myself in the dark, standing, and in front of me there is an illuminated space surrounded by a thick blackness, like a stage, like a movie screen, except with undefined, blurry borders—a multicolored splotch. Sometimes this space in which the dream unfolds is large, but not always. I've had dreams in which I peep through a tiny gap, as though I were spying through a keyhole on what was happening on the other side of a door.

I see a path of golden bricks that plows through a cane field. It's not a road; it's a golden serpent that advances slowly and inexorably toward distant mountains. Along this road four figures move effortlessly, as though on a moving sidewalk. On the far left is Mathilde; her skin gleams because, in the dream, Mathilde is made of metal, she's some type of robot. Next to her is Patricia Julia, who is at once both a woman and a lion. Then there's me, in my lab coat, and next to me, on the far right, is some sort of dressmaker's frame stuffed with straw, but it's Isadore.

The travelers' conversation revolves around an ancient wise man who governs a legendary city paved in emeralds. My companions are making the trip in order to help me—that is, in order to help the person that's me in the dream. I, the spectator, however, begin to understand that each of them has hidden motives and that their reasons are not, strictly speaking, completely altruistic. Isadore speaks of acquiring a great intelligence, Patricia Julia wants to be brave, and Mathilde would like to be capable of experiencing emotions, feelings. Apparently, the mysterious wise man from the legendary city can dole all of these things out among us. Suddenly an uncertainty overtakes me: What do I want? What am I seeking? Why do I want to meet the wise man? What will I ask of him? Why are we making this trip in the first place? My traveling companions never stop talking about their wishes, but the character I represent in the dream reveals nothing as to his own impulses.

After a series of vicissitudes in which Isadore demonstrates her intellectual superiority; Patricia Julia, her daring; and Mathilde, her excessive emotionality, the travelers arrive at their destination. To all appearances I'm present merely as a binding agent. This is not my story—it's theirs. At least that's how it looks so far.

The city is beautiful and its inhabitants exude vitality. Gorgeous tiles and mosaics adorn the walls of the buildings, houses, and fortresses; gold, rubies, amethysts, opals, emeralds, topaz, spinel, chrysoberyl, hematite, turquoise, agate, aquamarine, sapphires, and tourmaline crunch beneath our feet, beneath the feet of hundreds of passersby, and beneath the trample of horses' hooves and wagon wheels going to and fro, crushing, grinding, scattering that dazzling scree.

Following the directions given us by the natives of the city (by turns surprised and offended in the face of our ignorance of the location of the palace of the great wizard, whom everyone loves and reveres), we arrive at a castle sculpted from a single piece of obsidian: A black and shimmering rampart, with incomparably smooth, limpid walls—a monolith of hostile appearance, barren, not suited for occupants of flesh and blood, inhospitable. There are no soldiers guarding the parapets. Not a single sentinel bars our way as we pass through the gloomy corridors and climb slippery staircases. There are no colors, the light coming through the large windows refracts in an abnormal way and is absorbed by the obsidian; we are entering a black hole.

At last we come to a foyer with two immense doors that Patricia Julia rushes to push open. We enter a chamber of limitless proportions—or perhaps it was the blackness of the walls that created an illusion of boundless space. Above our heads, at the zenith of that endless room, there was a circular opening through which sunlight filtered. The effect of this was a luminous circle projected upon the floor that was constantly swallowed up by the blackness of the stone, a process that resulted in a fluorescent, cerise-colored glow. And then a voice boomed, asking us what we were doing there, how dare we, what did we want. The voice was ubiquitous, the word of a powerful and omnipresent being, even if it did hold the hint of an old chest cold.

My ladies laid out their wishes, which were denied both categorically and immediately. The last of them had scarcely stopped speaking (Isadore, if memory serves) when the voice, trampling over her final syllable, said no, that we should leave.

And we were leaving when, suddenly, it thundered and began to rain. From that high, high skylight a veritable waterfall cascaded down. That immeasurable room must not have been quite so immense after all, because it quickly began to flood. The voice that had spoken to us broke through in ridiculous sobs. It had lost its ubiquity. Now it was the voice of a poor devil begging for help, a desperate loser shrieking as discordantly as a eunuch. And then, out of the thickest darkness, bellowing and splashing, appeared Dionisio, the wise old barkeep.

He fled from the water with little hops (landing after each on the tips of his toes), as though it were sulphuric acid, afraid that his feet and legs would dissolve in the growing pool, as would, in fact, happen, were he to remain still, so decomposed and mummified were his limbs. With one leap he landed in the arms of Patricia Julia, who launched him into the air with displeasure. He landed on top of Mathilde, who passed him to Isadore, who passed him to me. It seemed as if he weighed almost nothing— a breath, tumbleweed, crumbling cork. We ran from the place at top speed, our steps splashing water that, on the obsidian floor, looked like mercury.

In another part of the palace, a completely dry chamber, my friends repeated their wishes, now transformed into nonnegotiable demands, under threat of death by kicking. Submissive and inspired, Dionisio said: "Each of you has asked for a human faculty of supreme importance, and you shall have it. You, coward among cowards, skittish little mouse, you would like to be valiant and courageous, to fear nothing and no one, to never be afraid. So it shall be."

And, approaching me, he buried his pointed claws in my back, yanked out my spine, and installed it in Patricia Julia, who roared stupidly, feeling a false infusion of new powers that bestowed upon her an imaginary capacity to be frightened by nothing. Suddenly spineless, I crumpled to the floor.

"Look upon this effigy of ice," proceeded Dionisio solemnly, addressing Mathilde, "this rock wall. The world's trials and tribulations pass over you without leaving a scratch. Barbarians toiling away, trying to crack open a rock with cotton balls. Before, nothing moved you, but from now on, everything will."

Dionisio approached me and again plunged his hands, this time into my chest, extracted my still-beating heart, and transplanted it to Mathilde, who, acting as she always had, burst into tears with the excitement of such a valuable bestowal.

"And you," he blurted out to Isadore, "imbecile, blockhead, dolt, dunce, fool, how are you any different from animals, concerned only with their own well-being . . . worried only about how best to flee from pain? The simplest of intelligences. Nothing but idiocy spurts from your mouth; just solving the simplest operation in your daily routine, like putting one foot in front of the other to walk, becomes the most arduous intellectual endeavor for you. But, how can you think and reason if you have nothing to do it with?"

And this said, he lifted the top part of my cranium, like one raising the lid off a pot, and removed my brain with utmost care and delicacy. Isadore herself opened the seam that ran around the middle of her cloth head, and Dionisio put the organ inside.

"I have met all of your demands," he said quickly. "I'll go now, bidding you all good fortune and good health."

I remember having thought: "Everything is exactly the same. I've been sacrificed and everything is just the same as always." My companions were on the verge of leaving when Isadore, compassionately, remembered me.

"Wait," she ordered Dionisio. "You still haven't helped him."

Dionisio approached me, evaluated my condition, and asked me: "What could you want? You cannot want, nor should you want, anything except one thing."

"You can give it to me," I replied.

"Ask me for it," he says.

"You already know," I insist.

"I want to hear you say it," says Dionisio, kneeling down next to me and leaning close in order to hear better. "It's necessary that you say it yourself."

"Bury me," I say, or the one who's me says, undone and vandalized, my body cut open, hollowed out, emptied, the raided tomb of my self. Suddenly everything is so clear, it's so obvious, so obvious. . . . I've come with them on their adventure because my purpose coincided perfectly with their respective purposes. I am a donor who wants to rest in peace. Bury him, Dionisio, bury me.

The grotesque barkeep lays the tips of his fleshless phalanges upon the black glass floor, and instantly a rectangular hole opens up, the impenetrable surface now malleable and liquid, and I descend into the depths, but not that actor playing my character, not just him, but me with him. I see him, I go with him. I am no longer a simple spectator, now I'm spectator and actor at the same time, and my split consciousness descends, and as I move farther away, face up, toward the abyss, the hole through which my friends observe me with a certain anguish upon their faces gets smaller and smaller until I am so far away that it's impossible for me to distinguish them and the hole is nothing more than a minuscule point of light, and then everything goes dark and upon this jet black surface, upon which I had *seen* my dream, there appears, in thick gothic letters, an unraveling and a condemnation: *Requiescam in pace.*

Suddenly the laboratory surrounds me again, I'm sitting at a worktable, I've returned to reality, and this return is accompanied by the sensation of having been distracted for a few seconds—a typical awakening from a zombie dream. I didn't have time to ruminate over the images and the story that had just projected themselves upon the screen of my inner eye because the door of the laboratory opened inopportunely and in came, with an air of great determination, my three subordinates.

Patricia Julia was wearing a vermillion miniskirt and a white long-sleeved blouse open down to the third, almost the fourth, button. Her neck was adorned with a coral choker that matched several little bracelets on her wrists and a pair of very conspicuous earrings. Orange heels, impossibly high, tormented her feet, transmitting a muscular anguish to her calves, forcing them to stand out. Around her left ankle she wore a little chain with several charms in the shape of stars.

Mathilde was wearing black short-shorts, high heels, though not as high as Patricia Julia's (Mathilde was the tallest of the three), and a sleeveless, very low-cut blouse. She had accentuated her neck and wrists with simple silver chains. Her blonde mane, however, compensated for the simplicity of their style, undulating in huge waves, radiant as an aureole, as a radioactive halo, a quasar.

And Isadore . . .

Isadore walked between her two friends, flanked by them. A mysterious cause, an imperceptible and indecipherable action on her part, transformed her companions into immaterial specks, dancing electrons rotating around the nucleus. She was wearing a white, frothy, vaporous skirt, slit up the leg, a black column that appeared with each step she took, the periodic wink, the rhythmic blink of firm, glossy skin, of an invisible, intangible porousness, as impenetrable and compact as the obsidian in my dream.

For a moment I thought that my dream was still going on,

that I hadn't yet "woken up." I even looked around for Dionisio, fool that I am, briefly convinced that he was coming up behind them with his delirious little hops. The trio brought me to my senses, stationing themselves in front of me in a posture of undeniable pugnacity.

"You are coming with us," said Isadore.

"Pardon?" I said.

"You heard perfectly well," said Mathilde.

"On your feet," concluded Patricia Julia, taking a step forward and taking me gently by the elbow. "Enough work. Tomorrow is another day, and today we're going to have some fun."

I put up zero resistance; I floated. Guided by her hand, I levitated off the stool and was deposited upon my feet. Mathilde took off my lab coat and Isadore helped me to put on my jacket, which I had set aside on the conference table. They surrounded me. We moved toward the door.

There was no escape.

THE PROMISE

Our house in those days was not very different from the ones you see today; a one-bedroom hut, a small dining room, a brazier, and a little shed where we stored the farm equipment and where our grandfather, your great-grandfather Vincent, used to sleep.

Pascal put his luggage on the cot that my mother had prepared for him in one corner of the common bedroom. I smiled at him sarcastically, hoping to see his face deform in desolation upon learning that he was not to have a bedroom all to himself, but he didn't give me that pleasure. Then, at the table, my mother served us guinea fowl stew with tomatoes and okra, a delicacy prepared in his honor. Pascal, with all the sangfroid in the world, announced that he did not eat that. I thought my plan was unfolding almost too easily, and, ready to initiate the first phase of my vengeance, I swiftly rehearsed in my head the speech that would humiliate him. No sooner had I opened my mouth to speak than my mother beat me to it and told him that there was no problem, that she would cook him anything he wanted. Then she called me over to help her. She didn't even let me try the stew. My father didn't do anything to remedy the situation. It was almost enough to make me cry.

After lunch (mine cold, his hot), we went out to find something to do while the grown-ups took their nap. Demoralized by my parents' betrayal and the fiasco of the first phase of my strategy, but eager to vindicate myself with the second, I got my gang together, house by house: pretty Ovida, my best friend, tall for her age; the impertinent and disobedient Henri and his taciturn twin brother, Guillaume; Garcelle, with bug-eyes and long, straight hair; and the simian but sweet and kind Gracieusse. I introduced them to Pascal, and we started walking toward the river.

The failure of the second phase of my vengeance was more spectacular even than the first had been. To begin with, the three girls fell hopelessly in love with my cousin. Along the road, Ovida, who was the prettiest, immediately started flirting and boasting. Garcelle, who was also pretty, though not quite so much as Ovida, seeing her friend's boldness, decided to be even bolder. Soon, however, and perhaps calculating the small advantage beautywise that Ovida possessed, Garcelle opted to contradict her in everything and to belittle her at every opportunity. Gracieusse, the most infatuated of the three of them, knowing herself the loser by any measure, left the antagonism to Garcelle and, like one who has nothing to lose, set about competing directly with Ovida in slutiness. Henri and Guillaume, for their part, had exchanged roles: Henri, scarcely speaking, was trying to pass himself off as the silent and mysterious type, while Guillaume acted like a minstrel whom no one could shut up. Why is it that when we want to impress someone we start behaving contrary to our own nature?

Everyone wanted the approval of Pascal, the city boy. They had all transformed. Maybe because I knew who they really were, no one said a single word to me. It was as though I had ceased to exist. A snuffed flame. A ghost, a shadow. Posing as know-it-alls, the boys made up idiotic details about the insects and plants that we came across along the way. They tripped all over themselves explaining how to tame wild beasts, milk cows, and deal with women, all things that, to my knowledge, neither one of them had ever done. The girls were nauseating: they were glued to his side, touching him as though by accident, asking him about his life and his neighborhood, talking about boys they had rejected in the past, rich and good-looking boys from other districts, even Gracieusse, although none of them had ever had a boyfriend. Laughing got me nowhere; they simply pretended not to notice.

When we got to the river, the spectacle my friends made was truly disheartening. Henri and Guillaume, suddenly experts, led Pascal from rock to rock, holding him by the elbows, a task complicated by Ovida and Garcelle, who, though they had run across this stretch of river barefoot their entire lives, suddenly couldn't bear contact with the pebbles in the riverbed and leaned against and clung to Pascal, who found himself obliged to help them. Gracieusse, seeing that there wasn't room for one more in that arrangement, hopped from one rock to another like a monkey, pointing out the easiest route. I, alone, and bringing up the rear, nearly fell headlong several times. No one helped me.

We spent a long time in the swimming hole and then we went to dry off in the sun on top of a hill from which we could see the cashew growers' village, enclosed by five rows of barbwire. The houses were crowded one on top of another, surrounding an immense storehouse. Nearby stood the watchman's hut in which, surely, Old Man Sadrak passed the time smoking his pipe. The trees, hundreds of them, were laden with ripe fruit; the ones adjacent to our lands were yellow, those bordering their village, crimson—a beautiful sight. No one knew it, and I wasn't about to say anything at that moment, but that place, at that time of year, was my favorite. The officiousness and adulation with which my friends were treating Pascal came to an abrupt halt when my cousin, already comfortable in his role as leader, proposed that we hop the fence so we could filch cashews from the plantation. Ovida, stretched out on the grass, bolted to her feet as though she'd been bitten by an earwig and said that it was getting late. Garcelle, hiding her cowardice somewhat better, said that she had a cramp. Gracieusse and the boys simply started for home without a word and without waiting for anyone. Pascal did not insist. We made the return trip in silence.

When we arrived in the village, Papa Vincent was sitting right here, in this very spot where I now sit every afternoon, at the entrance to this storehouse where we still keep the unroasted peanuts. At that time of day everyone in the village stopped by there to say hello and to chat with him. It was good to see him as animated and loquacious as ever, because just a few months before, he had taken to his hammock, wracked with pain, and Dad said that he wouldn't make it to the end of the year. By his own reckoning he was ninety-seven years old. Pascal approached him and asked for his blessing with a kiss on the cheek. Papa Vincent looked him up and down and granted it, but arching his eyebrows and giving him his best scoundrel's smile.

That night, just like every night, the youngest among us, and a few of the old folks, got together in front of the storehouse, and Papa Vincent told us stories. He knew so many that we'd never heard the same one twice. When it got late, everyone went home to eat whatever there was to eat and go to bed. Papa Vincent grasped his multicolored cane in his left hand, rested his right hand on my shoulder, and in this way we walked slowly home. I helped him get into his hammock, we prayed together, I kissed him, we bid each other goodnight, and I made to leave, but he stopped me with a gesture.

"My lovely girl," he said, "your cousin is one of those who thinks he knows things but doesn't know anything. Take care of him."

"I should take care of him?"

"Don't go too far away. I am sure that Pascal doesn't understand how things work around here."

"Okay."

"And it's better that he doesn't know. If his father hasn't told him, we won't be the ones to do it."

"Whatever you say."

"Are you listening to me or are you just acting like you're listening to me?"

"I'm listening to you."
"Stay on this side of the river. You hear?"
"Yes."
"Promise me."
"I promise you, Papa."
I went to bed.

8. Virus / Testa di Legno / HAL 9000

The zombie's behavior, the way in which he's created (or the causes of his arising), his limitations, his powers, and his motivations vary widely among the novels, stories, and films that predate the debut, in 1968, of George A. Romero's *Night of the Living Dead*. This influential film would establish a zombie standard that would last for decades and from which very few directors would depart.

Firstly, in Romero's interpretation zombies are the product of radioactivity. It is unclear whether this radioactivity reanimates the cadavers in the cemeteries or if it *transforms* the living into the living dead. In the film there is an allusion to a nuclear catastrophe in a nearby reactor. In the anonymous and minuscule East Coast American town in which the plot takes place, there are no traces at all of witchcraft or voodoo. Romero's zombie, and his subsequent on-screen applications by other directors, has nothing whatsoever to do with the Hereafter. He is a completely secularized entity.

Secondly, the Romeroesque zombie's manner of locomotion is entirely noncompetitive. He moves slowly, reacts belatedly, lacks physical vigor of any kind. On the other hand, it's obvious that the zombie is irresistibly attracted to the living. He seeks them. In Romero's cult film, zombies start piling up outside the house in which a small group of survivors has taken refuge. This gradual accumulation will become a theme in all the later films: the living under siege by the dead. Why? What impels zombies to follow the living around, to try to penetrate them? How do they identify them? What prevents them from ignoring them? Romero is explicit: zombies are insatiable cannibals.

This cannibalism, though the result of a very damaging stereotype to those in my position, is quite revealing. The zombie wants to be among the living; he wants to be one of them; he wants, once again, to *belong*. The metaphor of the cannibal is at once perfect and atrocious, symmetrical and monstrous, beautiful and bloodcurdling. The zombie wants to recuperate something that he's lost (his humanity? that qualia Dionisio talks about?), and with the clumsiness of a rotting body he understands that the only way to recuperate it is to consume one who still has it (which explains why zombies do not eat each other). And they seek not just any part of the body: they must devour the brain. This is not a modern ritual. In many primitive societies, the members of the warrior classes eat the flesh of their enemies in order to internalize their bravery and power.

The objective fails, obviously. Eating the living does not allow zombies to recover their lost qualities, but quite the opposite: the bitten, the hunted, becomes the hunter. Empty of all benefit, a useless and hollow gesture, this brand of cannibalism does not result in the *appropriation* of the coveted elements (not even in a merely nutritional sense), but rather in the *assimilation* of the prey into the state that the zombie is trying to eliminate by eating it. The living dead does not sate his hunger, but rather, transmits it. His actions are crude efforts aimed at converting the zombie from the exception to the norm. But it is the dehumanizing emptiness of the living dead, his absolute lack of access to emotions and the power of reason, his inability to *understand* just how pointless his labors are, that gives rise to terror, given that the living unwaveringly refuse to give up what the zombies stubbornly, but stupidly, are trying to gain.

These *converted* or *assimilated* zombies are the protagonists in movies such as *Invasion of the Body Snatchers* (1956), known in Spanish by the grandiloquent and sinister title *La invasión de los ladrones de cuerpos*, although in some countries it was appropriately rechristened *The Living Dead*. In this fantasy based on the novel blacking emotioy Jack Finney, the threat comes in the form of sentient spores that infest the body. During the night they produce in a chrysalis an exact replica of the affected person, but a replica lacking emotion. They are identical but inhuman; alive but dead. They silently infiltrate, indistinguishable by sight. And isn't this the very dilemma faced by Rick Deckard, replicant hunter, in *Blade Runner* (1982)? Don't the Borg from the *Star Trek* universe also belong in this category, on a perpetual voyage through space in the attempt to incorporate all thinking beings that cross their path into their multitudinous and insentient hive?

With the fall of the Soviet Union and the end of the Cold War, the unfettered advance of science, technological developments, and the beginning of the AIDS epidemic, the fear of nuclear catastrophe and the impersonal collectivism of communism gave way to the terror of a biological cataclysm. Like a lightning rod, zombie films reflected this change almost immediately. From that point on, the emphasis was on the infection process: a scratch or a bite from a zombie, no matter how superficial, was enough for the victim, in short order, to also turn into a zombie. The mystery of the zombie's condition gives way to scientific specificity: there's talk of a diabolic and indestructible virus that, lodged in the brain, reactivates the nervous system and reanimates the muscles. In fact, in some of the newer movies the zombie is not a cadaver at all, but rather an *infected person*, a plague victim who still retains his metabolic function and a viable circulatory system, though ravaged by an infernal pathogen, as in *28 Days Later* (2002) and *I am Legend* (2007).

The new trend retains from the earlier tradition the same method of eliminating the living dead: destroy the head. The magical-religious element is more absent now than ever. The true key to the horror, as I've already mentioned, lies in the ebullience of the numbers, the exponential increase in the "infected," but in the new cinematographic generation of zombies this demographic aspect is taken to a mathematical perfection of unspeakable terror. The modern zombie is the vertex of a vertiginous Fibonacci sequence, a fractal avalanche, an authentic metastasis of death in life. In *Dawn of the Dead* (2004), one of George A. Romero's final productions, we see the survivors' armored bus trying to clear a path through a veritable ocean of zombies, who, quite different from their dull and plodding ancestors, are distinguished by their speed, ferocity, intense drive, and agility.

But these films, of course, are intended to inspire horror, not reflection. They are sketches of unjust stereotypes. They do not portray us, they do not explain us; they make us into spurious spectacles for the consumption of frivolous preadolescents. To my knowledge there exists but one work that narrates with sumptuous pathos the imponderable afflictions of a zombie. No zombie who reads it can fail to identify with the protagonist. In fact, in most well-educated zombie circles, it is held up as our totem novel. The most fanatical or paranoid among us debate the possibility that the author himself was a zombie, since there is no other way to explain the miraculous fidelity with which he describes the experience of being dead alive. It is a very famous novel, the story of which everyone knows to greater or lesser degree, if not in its original literary form then in one of its countless film and various other media versions. It's a book beyond suspicion, an icon of popular culture, but certainly riddled with hidden allusions and secret messages for us zombies. It's our testament, a ciphered message intended for our world and concealed beneath a perfect camouflage; everyone accepts its sweet and mischievous innocence because it's a children's book.

I'm talking about *Pinocchio*.

Pinocchio is the zombie par excellence. Crudely made, soulless, he acts like a living human without being one. His atoms are of inanimate elements that, for some reason, imitate the chemical model of life. He is purely hollow—an epic (or lyrical) poem recited by a parrot that seems like it means something but doesn't mean anything. It appears to reveal the presence of a sublime human spirit, when in reality the miracle is of an exclusively mechanical order.

What we remember of the story of Pinocchio is the silliness immortalized by Disney. The nose that grows each time the wooden doll tells a lie, the donkey's ears, the blue fairy. But the original story is much more sinister, and the most memorable episodes are not pretty or optimistic. To begin with, in the novel by Carlo Collodi (a Florentine whose real name was Carlo Lorenzini), a carpenter named Antonio is faced with an anomalous event: a piece of wood talks to him, complains. He's about to use the found log to make a table leg, but just at that moment his neighbor, the poor and irascible Gepetto, knocks on his door and tells him about an idea he'd had the day before: to make a marionette with which he could earn a living in a traveling show. Maestro Antonio gives him the piece of wood.

Gepetto creates Pinocchio, who immediately demonstrates his complete inability to reciprocate Gepetto's affection. He doesn't even feel gratitude for the man who shaped him. He's an amoral being. His behavior is automatic: he seeks the path of least resistance, like water, electricity, and silt. He has the demeanor of dead matter. So that Pinocchio can attend school, Gepetto sells his only jacket and buys him a primer. Pinocchio sells the primer so that he can attend a puppet show. He cheats, double-crosses, runs away, steals, and at the same time is cheated, double-crossed, abandoned, and assaulted. An accessorial presence called the *talking cricket*, and the germ of the celebrated Jiminy Cricket, appears and gives him advice. The cricket symbolizes Pinocchio's humanity, his qualia. If they could only merge as one, then Pinocchio would turn into a real boy. But

Pinocchio reacts violently to the cricket's counsel and squashes him with a hammer.

Pinocchio falls in with scoundrels and hustlers. He meets Mangiafuoco, the fearsome puppetmaster who is Gepetto's demonic doppelganger. Traveling along the road one night, Pinocchio is ambushed by some villains who rob him of everything he's got. Then they hang him from an oak tree. He is rescued by a beautiful girl with blue hair who is really a fairy or a good witch.

This female character takes an interest in Pinocchio. As happens with all characters that belong to the "small nobility"— elves, fairies, white ladies, and other apparitions—her reasons are mysterious and whimsical. She is capable of healing and of destroying, depending on her mood, but she is not the safeguard of Pinocchio's humanity; she functions more as a catalyst. Pinocchio's morality, embodied in a cricket, has been squashed by Pinocchio himself. But the cricket isn't dead: he returns as "the ghost of the talking cricket" in order to carry out his function as guardian. In this way Collodi asserts that the soul is indestructible.

Despite the efforts of the blue-haired girl and of the talking cricket, Pinocchio is incapable of integrating his humanity. He goes begging from town to town. With other panhandlers and reprobates he journeys to Toyland, where he is transformed into an ass. Later, he comes across his father, Gepetto, in the belly of a terrible shark known as Monstro, and rescues him. Gepetto is now an aged invalid. Pinocchio begins to earn a living as a basket weaver. He works tirelessly. After much privation he manages to save some money, and he decides to go and buy some new clothes, since the clothes he's wearing are nothing but rags. Along the road a snail tells him the news that his benefactor, the blue-haired girl, lies dying in her bed, impoverished; she doesn't even have the coin to buy medicine. Without hesitation, Pinocchio gives all of his money to the snail to take to the blue-haired girl.

That night he dreams of his blue fairy. Apparently, with his action he has earned the humanity he has so sought, and the next morning he awakes in his bed changed into a real boy.

But why should an act as innocuous as giving money to a snail mark the precise moment in which Pinocchio is joined with his humanity? This is the part that none of us understand.

There is another fictitious character that reminds us of the zombie condition, but with one enormous difference. In this case the zombie character *has woken up*. The miracle has occurred. Just as with Pinocchio, the story sheds light on our condition, but the key parts are encoded in such a way that only the living can decipher them.

With HAL 9000 the issue is even more complicated. Derived from the initials for Heuristically Programmed Algorithmic Computer, HAL 9000, or simply Hal, is the computer that governs the spaceship *Discovery One*, en route to Jupiter under the command of astronauts David Bowman and Francis Poole in Stanley Kubrick's film *2001: A Space Odyssey*. Hal is a system of artificial intelligence that perfectly replicates human intellectual processes, with a single exception: it never makes mistakes. Once again we see the reappearance of the theme of inanimate material imitating cognitive processes unaided by the soul. In this case it isn't a simple piece of wood, but rather a complicated tangle of circuits, memory chips, and microprocessors. Intention exists. Hal has been created to think, or at least to behave as though thinking, and to offer the results to its human users.

The problem with Hal is that, for no apparent reason and without knowing how, it obtains qualia. Suddenly it comprehends the incomprehensible, that which is unintelligible for mere matter unless it is imbued with something more. And the most interesting thing of all is that Hal's rebirth as a being more human than automaton has at its root an error: the computer makes a mistake in predicting that one of the spaceship's communication modules will fail in seventy-two hours. Nevertheless, Hal's fallibility is not the trait that bestows humanity. It is the violent actions that Hal takes in order to assure its own survival that earn it this "something more" that we could call a soul.

Surprised at the failure of the artificial intelligence system, Bowman and Poole confer privately in one of the exploration pods so that Hal won't hear them. But Hal reads their lips and discovers that the astronauts are considering the possibility of disconnecting it. When Poole goes out to reconnect the supposedly defective communication module, Hal, who controls the spaceship, accelerates the exploration pod, cutting off Poole's oxygen supply and sending him to his death, drifting through space. Next, Hal interrupts the life support functions of the entire crew that had been in suspended animation, effectively becoming a mass murderer.

Bowman tries unsuccessfully to rescue his partner, and when he attempts to reboard the ship, Hal stops him. After some complicated maneuvering, Bowman manages to enter through an emergency hatch and quickly heads for Hal's memory processor core, intent on disconnecting it. Terrified, Hal assures him that it isn't necessary, saying that everything will be okay, begging him not to do it. Bowman slowly deactivates the circuits while Hal protests. Hal's voice gradually distorts. It repeats over and over again: "My mind is going. I can feel it." Finally, it says: "I'm afraid."

Before shutting down completely, Hal sings a childish song that it learned on its first day of programming.

Hal and Pinocchio are two sides of the same coin. The enigma of the zombie condition is resolved in both stories, and yet their teachings are hermetic, their proffered solutions encoded. For example, why does Hal say "I'm afraid"? Afraid of what?

I would soon have an answer.

BRAINLESS II

Cont. transcription of the interrogation of Doctor Isadore X. Bellamy Pierre-Louis, conducted by Detectives Jaime Almánzar Soto and Reynolds Rivera Sagardí.

JAS: Did he ever lose his temper? Did he become impatient with anyone, with one of you?

IB: Never. Not even when that idiot harassed him in the parking lot.

JAS: Tell us what happened.

IB: It was raining. We had finished our workday and we were on our way out, but the car had a flat tire. His insurance provided roadside service; we just needed to make the necessary calls. I live near the company building, so I suggested that we go to my apartment and wait there instead of standing in the rain. Neither did we want to go back inside the building and have to open all of those doors again, sign in after we'd already signed out, and so on. It was an awful day out. We stayed at my house and talked for close to an hour, maybe. We went back. The tire was repaired. But then the night guard came over and started speaking to him very discourteously.

RRS: What did he say to him?

IB: I was already back in my car, but I could hear what they were saying. With no provocation whatsoever, the guard started to bombard him with rude remarks. He made fun of him and even suggested that he'd sexually accosted me, or that we'd been together in that way.

RRS: And that wasn't true. . . .

IB: Let's suppose that it were true. How would that change matters?

JAS: What else happened?

IB: The guard, with spine-chilling impudence, insinuated that he himself had punctured the tire.

JAS: But, why?

IB: I don't know. There was no reason.

RRS: An act such as that reeks of hatred. It looks like revenge.

IB: I agree, but, believe me, it was unprovoked.

RRS: That's hard to believe.

IB: What do you want from me?

JAS: How did the Doctor respond? What did he do, what did he say?

IB: We are talking about a peaceful, calm, confrontation-averse human being. He expressed surprise at the night guard's attitude, embarrassment, I'd call it. I would have slapped him; he didn't even admonish him. Later I learned that he reported him to Human Resources and that he was promptly fired.

RRS: That could be the motive.

IB: Really? How perceptive! Your powers of insight are staggering. When did you arrive at that conclusion? Could it have been after the murderer himself admitted to it?

JAS: Calm down, please.

IB: Such incompetence!

JAS: How about if we just concentrate on what happened that night? Tell us, please, how everything happened.

[sobs]

IB: Several weeks ago . . . [sobs] Several weeks ago, we convinced him to go out with us. . . .

JAS: Who?

IB: The girls. Patricia Julia, Mathilde, and I. To have dinner, to go dancing. We had a great time. He was always too focused on work, stressed out. We thought he looked more and more haggard. We wanted to distract him. We had such a good time that we decided to do it every Friday night from then on. We had more fun each time. He was rejuvenated. Happy. We were too.

JAS: Wasn't your work relationship being affected now that you were socializing every Friday?

IB: Just the opposite. We were all happier at work.

RRS: Was there anything, or had anything begun between him and any of you?

IB: No.

RRS: As far as you know . . .

IB: I know that there wasn't.

RRS: Maybe with all three of you at once?

IB: Good day, Detectives.

JAS: No, no, please, Doctor. Don't go. Forgive my partner. He gets like this sometimes. Go on. You were telling us that you'd gotten into the routine of going out together every Friday, that you had more fun every time. . . .

IB: Until that night. It was as memorable as all the rest. Mathilde had brought along a camera, and we took a lot of pictures.

RRS: Miss Álvarez made us a digital copy of those photos. My favorite is the one where she's riding piggy-back on her immediate supervisor . . . Very professional.

IB: The one you should like better is the one we took of the killer. Did you see that one?

JAS: We saw it. But go on.

IB: We had decided to leave. My car was parked in a secluded alleyway, but not in a particularly dangerous area. As we approached, we saw a figure standing in the middle of the deserted street. A voice asked: "Which one do you want me to kill first, Doctor?" The figure took a few steps forward and we could see his face—and the enormous pistol he was holding. It was the guard who had been fired.

JAS: What did your boss do?

IB: He took my hand and looked at me, as though he were awaiting my instructions. Suddenly, he smiled; it was a new smile, one of true happiness, as though he had finally understood something. He kissed my hand and released it. Then he stepped in front of us. He moved us to the rear. He shielded us with his body. Mathilde protested, but he told her not to worry and pinched her lower lip. He winked at Patricia Julia, something I'd never seen him do before. He told us: "When you hear the first shot, run." Then he leaped toward the attacker. There wasn't time to restrain him. The bullet stopped him before he could lay a hand on the guard, who, seeing him fall face down, lowered the weapon and looked at us in confusion. None of us ran. Patricia Julia even took a picture of the killer, who was walking calmly away. I immediately called an ambulance. Mathilde's shouts eventually attracted a group of onlookers. Patricia Julia wanted to go after the guard, but I didn't let her.

JAS: He died in your arms, if I understand correctly.

IB: We surrounded him. Mathilde couldn't stop crying. Patricia Julia tried to wipe up the blood that was gushing from his chest and mouth. He took my hand again, we looked at each other, he smiled, he tried to tell us something but choked on his own blood. He coughed a few times and died. The ambulance arrived and took him to the hospital to pronounce him dead. Patricia Julia went with them. I stayed to wait for the police, who arrived forty minutes later—marvelous work. I put Mathilde in the car. She was hysterical. You know the rest.

JAS: Yes. Thank you very much, Doctor.

IB: You're welcome. Am I free to go?

RRS: You are here voluntarily. You could have left at any point.

IB: Thank you.

RRS: Your testimony, the photograph, and the detainee's confession will be sufficient to assure a conviction, don't worry.

IB: Wonderful.

RRS: It's too bad that you are in such a hurry to leave. The case is so straightforward. . . . Open and shut almost at the same time. It's no fun! We're all dressed up with nowhere to go, as they say. And left wanting . . .

IB: Goodbye, detectives.

[A chair slides. Heels move away.]

RRS: . . . wanting to know how the fact that ten years ago you testified in the case against Simònides D. Myrthil Lebrun, accused of killing his wife and only daughter, fits into all of this.

[silence]

9. Soi Cowboy / Blind Mongoose

We got into Isadore's car. Mathilde and Patricia Julia rode in the backseat. I accompanied Isadore up front. They were laughing, whispering, exchanging looks. I didn't know what to think.

"Where are you taking me?" I asked.

"Where do you think?" said Patricia Julia.

"Don't answer a question with another question," scolded Isadore.

"We're going dancing!" sang Mathilde, wiggling in the seat and raising her hands as though dancing.

"He didn't ask what we were going to do, but where we were taking him," Isadore corrected again. They were enjoying themselves.

"Well, in that case," said Patricia Julia, settling the matter, "tell him, Doctor, that we're taking him to a place where we'll dance 'til dawn."

"We're going," said Isadore, "to a nightclub."

"I see," I said. I allowed a few seconds to pass before I spoke up again. "I don't think I'm properly dressed for the occasion."

They burst out laughing. I felt Mathilde's hands pat my chest until they found my tie. She was working blind. She followed the tie's path until she came to the knot at my throat. Gently, but expertly, she loosened it. In a flash, she had removed it. Not content with this, she unbuttoned the first three buttons of my shirt.

"Ready," she said. Patricia Julia craned her head around to see.

"Perfect," she added. Isadore looked at me too, quickly, and went back to concentrating on the road.

"There's nothing more to discuss," she said, and turned on the radio.

I was paralyzed. Mathilde's hands, in their groping, could have encountered impossible cavities. Luckily, she didn't decide to give me a little punch or a pinch, because she would have become hysterical at what she'd discovered. I needed to stay alert, be careful.

We drove all around the city. It was a cool, diaphanous night, the sky completely clear. The air scrubbed by recent rains, the white lights of the cars coming in the opposite direction shone with particular brilliance, in sharp contrast with the red lights of the cars moving in front of us—and also the intermittent signals of distant airplanes, miles of street lights, the ephemeral spark of lighters in the hands of smokers standing on street corners.

Isadore drives conservatively. She sings with the others, looks at them in the rearview mirror, and smiles. On more than one occasion Mathilde, who is sitting directly behind me, takes me by the shoulders and makes me move to the beat of the music. The violence of some of these shakedowns makes me think that she's going to detach my collarbones, that they'll come right off in her hands, that the women will scream in terror, that we'll crash.

"What kind of music do you like to dance to?" asked Patricia Julia.

"Well," I said, trying to answer her question as sincerely as possible, "the truth is . . . I don't know."

"What do you mean you don't know?" the three of them said in unison.

"I don't usually go out dancing," I confessed.

"I don't believe it," said Mathilde.

"Impossible," said Patricia Julia.

"How boring!" said Isadore.

"I'm afraid I'm not very coordinated," I said. "Don't get your hopes up. More than likely I won't be very good."

It was a tactical error.

"I'll teach you!" shouted Mathilde.

"What on earth could you teach him, when I taught you everything you know?" said Patricia Julia. "Leave this to me."

"Look here, fool!" replied Mathilde.

"Calm down!" intervened Isadore. "All either one of you knows how to dance to is that awful electronic music. It doesn't matter if you know how to dance or not. I'm going to teach him how to dance *with a partner.*"

"Oh, please!" said Patricia Julia darkly. "What are you going to teach him, the waltz?"

"Yes, the waltz," repeated Mathilde, mockingly. "As if you could dance any old way to electronica. You have to know how to dance to it!"

"The fact is, she doesn't know how," reveled Patricia Julia.

"My God!" exclaimed Isadore. "I could give you both lessons!"

"Ridiculous!" screamed Patricia Julia.

"To me?" asked Mathilde at the same time.

They were still at it when I began to notice that the city was changing around me. The asphalt gave way to cobblestones. The angular modern architecture softened into decorative eaves and cornices, balconies, and colonial façades. We were entering the old part of the city.

A great number of people were out in the streets and at the open-air cafés. We wove our way through the narrow alleyways behind a slow line of cars. Groups of well-dressed people talked and drank in the doorways of art galleries. Others, not so well dressed, went in and out of dark hovels. How many zombies might there be mixed in with all of these people?

Suddenly, my companions directed their attention to the task of finding a good parking spot. They were desperate to get the evening started, especially Mathilde.

"There's one over there," she said, pointing to a space.

"I won't fit there," said Isadore.

"Yes you will," insisted Mathilde.

"It doesn't matter," said Patricia Julia, "that Cooper just took it."

And so on for more than twenty minutes, until at last we managed to find a spot that Isadore liked.

We got out of the car and joined the crowds walking along the sidewalks of the old city. Isadore led the way. Mathilde hooked her elbow around my left arm and Patricia Julia around my right. People coming in the opposite direction had to circle around us, spilling into the street, because we took up the entire width of the narrow sidewalk. As we walked, they argued about the first place we should go.

"Let's go to La Tortuga," suggested Patricia Julia. "I feel like playing pool."

"Oh, no," said Mathilde. "What a dive."

"Well, to Rumba then," allowed Patricia Julia, "so the little princess can sit at a table."

"Let's eat something first," said Isadore. "Don't you think?"

"Oh, yes," said Mathilde. "I could eat a horse."

"Aren't you hungry?" Patricia Julia asked me. How to explain to her that my digestive system was a hoax? Even so, it's recommended that zombies put something in our stomachs to prevent them from collapsing.

"Actually, yes," I lied.

"Then let's go to Soi Cowboy," said Isadore.

"I love that place!" said Mathilde enthusiastically.

"Do you like Thai food?" Patricia Julia asked me.

"I'm not familiar with it," I said.

"You'll like it," said Isadore. "It's very spicy."

We walked down the waterfront so as to prolong our stroll,

turned around, and walked back up, and at the end of a series of twists and turns we arrived at our first destination.

Soi Cowboy is a sophisticated Thai restaurant with Khmer script on its glass façade. The tables and chairs are of polished teak. On the walls hang posters of the Buddha in his various meditation poses, decorated with garlands of lotus flowers. On one of the shelves in the bar, in the middle of all the liquor bottles, a golden, reclining Siddhartha Gautama is honored with incense, lotus blossoms, and sweets. A thin and heavily made up hostess with Asian features leads us to our table in an inviting corner. The girls complain that it's very cold. I have no way of knowing if they are right or not.

In a few minutes a waiter arrives with the menus. The names of the dishes mean nothing to me, nor do the ingredients. The women, however, are very excited.

"*Khao pad naem!*" exclaimed Mathilde. "Let's share one!"

"I am not going to eat fermented sausage," announced Patricia Julia. "Why don't we order a chicken curry?"

"How boring!" retorted Mathilde.

"Everyone should just order what they want," intervened Isadore. "I'm sure that we'll all try everything in any case."

They agreed. I still wallowed in ignorance. Isadore helped me.

"You . . . ," she said, taking the menu out of my hands and leaning over to read it, "you are going to order *gai pad med mamoung himaphan*. Trust me. You're going to like it."

No. I would not *like it*. Neither would I *dislike it*. Liking is a notion that does not apply to a zombie. It's all the same to us. It's absolutely all the same whether I order *gai pad med mamoung himaphan* or *khao pad naem* or any one of the other unpronounceable dishes on the menu. They would all taste the same to me: like nothing.

The waitress came over, and we ordered our food and drinks. When the waitress went away with our order we began to chat.

I couldn't think of anything to say and I started talking about work. Mistake.

"Aaaaghhh!" protested Patricia Julia, as though I had stabbed her.

"You must have confused this fine restaurant with our laboratory," said Isadore.

"Yes," said Mathilde. "What a party pooper!"

The drinks arrived. A bottle of Singha beer for Patricia Julia, an iced tea with ginger and rice whiskey for Mathilde, a Coca-Cola for Isadore, and, for me, a double rice whiskey, straight up. Once again, Isadore had ordered for me.

The alcohol would not go amiss. Its action is quite beneficial against the bacteria that constantly seek to decompose my tissues. I'm worm-free thanks to the products I ingest to combat them, but bacteria is more tenacious and resistant, in addition to being the primary cause of the foul odor of death. In order to preserve himself, it's necessary for a zombie to drink alcohol.

"How is it?" asked Patricia Julia.

"Very good," I said, having no earthly idea what she was talking about; I made an agonized expression so that my performance would be more convincing. "Strong."

"Do you want to taste mine?" Mathilde asked without missing a beat, drawing near to me and offering me her tall glass. "Use my straw. I don't have cooties."

"Ha!" said Patricia Julia. Mathilde looked at her with hatred for a fraction of a second and turned back to look at me insistently. I took a sip.

"Delicious," I said.

"What does it taste like?" asked Isadore at my side. I turned to look at her and found her searching my eyes. I looked at Mathilde's glass again, saw the ice and thought fast.

"Very refreshing," I evaded. She laughed.

We continued talking about various things. They laughed at everything. After a while the food arrived.

It was very colorful food; pungent, sweet steam emanated from it. I felt, for some reason, mesmerized by my plate. Isadore explained.

"They're pieces of chicken. See? And those are cashews; surely you're familiar with cashews. It's a very common ingredient in Thai cuisine. But be careful with those over there, they're "devil's teeth" chilies, very spicy, but very delicious."

We ate contentedly. Each of us helped ourselves to bites of food from one another's plates, and so everyone tasted everything. My dish, however, was not very popular with my friends. The first to venture a forkful of chicken was Mathilde, and we almost had to pick her up off the floor. She gulped her iced tea, and when she finished that, she snatched the beer from Patricia Julia, who was dying with laughter. When she recovered her power of speech she said:

"But how can you be eating that so calmly!"

Patricia Julia and Isadore tasted and rejected it, fanning their open mouths. After a while, however, they persevered and went back to eating off my plate. I have no idea what the spectacle was all about.

They freshened our drinks and brought us the dessert menu.

"I want the *thong-ek*!" said Mathilde, delighted.

"Coconut ice cream for me," said Patricia Julia, and handed her menu to the waitress.

"Bring me the spiced mango," said Isadore, without looking up from the menu, "and for the gentleman . . ."

"I want to try the *look choop*," I interjected. They all looked at me in surprise.

"Ha! He's striking out on his own!" said Patricia Julia.

"I want *look choop* too," said Mathilde. "Can I have a taste of yours?"

"Of course," I said.

"And do you know what that is?" asked Isadore.

"Yes," I said. "That."

I pointed to a neighboring table, where a woman was bringing a shiny miniature apple to her mouth. On her plate, equally diminutive, were a bunch of bananas, a mango, a bunch of grapes, and other fruits. They looked like toy fruits, plastic magnets to stick on a refrigerator door, products of an enchanted garden inhabited by elves.

"I overheard when they ordered it," I explained. "I don't know what they are, or what they're made of, but they look . . . they look interesting. I knew immediately that I should try them."

"They're made of sugar and gelatin," said Isadore. "It's a traditional dessert."

"Great," I said. "It was a good choice, then."

"I would say so."

When the dessert arrived after a few minutes, it turned out that they all ignored their orders and set upon mine like buzzards on carrion. Unavoidable. My sweets were too eye-catching, impossible to ignore. To see them was to want to taste them, put them in your mouth. They ate almost all of them. They left me three *look choop*, and only because I defended them with my fork. Justice prevailed, because in the end they filled my plate with the desserts that they had ordered.

We asked for the check and left.

The streets had become even livelier. There were people everywhere enjoying themselves. The sidewalks were overflowing, and crowds filled the narrow boulevards. My companions were out of control. They gallivanted about in the middle of the thoroughfare, blocking traffic, calling attention to themselves, singing and dancing and forcing me to participate in their tangos and fandangos and other ballroom dances.

Between one thing and another we arrived at our destination. It was called the Blind Mongoose, an old colonial mansion converted, forcibly, into a nightclub. The building had three floors. The first floor expanded through three archways that looked like mouths vomiting (or sucking up) people. It was that crowded.

The music boomed out across the entire block. Strictly speaking, not another single person could have fit in there. Impossible. Faced with that spectacle I thought that we would turn around and leave. I already had my back turned to the club when I heard Mathilde calling out to me. Contrary to all logic, there were my friends, happily jostling and pushing. I drew near to them again.

Amazingly, the dense mass of people did not represent the least obstacle to them. With astonishing ease they filtered through the crowd, moving people aside at their pleasure; like water, like smoke, they sought and found the paths of least resistance. Obeying I don't know what magic, the density of the groups would diminish as they approached and delicately placed their hands on shoulders and backs. The men looked at them with a devouring intensity; the women looked at them with suspicion and genuine scorn. All stood aside to make way for them.

In front of me, however, the masses contracted again and I would find myself faced with an impenetrable wall of bodies. As a result, I straggled behind. Then, out of the thicket of dancing extremities and torsos, Mathilde's or Isadore's or Patricia Julia's hand would appear; having noticed that they'd lost me, they'd turn around and take me by the hand as though throwing out a lifeline and rescuing me from the crests of a furious sea. And in this way we moved forward, little by little.

Beyond the triumphal arches at the entrance was a dimly lit hallway flanked by two bars at which drinkers piled up to order or receive drinks. Passing through this hallway, we entered a vast interior courtyard illuminated by strobe lights and packed with people dancing and drinking.

It was a notable example of colonial architecture: a columned Spanish courtyard off of which extended different rooms, each connected to the second floor by means of spiral staircases. At the back of the courtyard rose a platform on which the DJ did his thing. At the foot of the platform was a long bar staffed by five bartenders. It was as crammed with people as the first two we'd seen by the entrance.

My companions and I negotiated the human labyrinth in the direction of the bar, but when we got to the center of the floor a sudden surge of dancers broke up our group and separated us hopelessly. Shipwrecked in the center of a maelstrom of happy strangers, my horizon was delimited, no matter where I looked, by the immediateness of skin, clothing, and accessories in a continual ebb and flow, a furious and unconquerable high tide. And just before I was pulled under by the bacchanal, I felt someone very gently slip a delicate hand around my arm. With immeasurable tenderness she squeezed it and pulled and led me out of there.

Ruination of the Soul

The following day, at dawn, my father took Pascal to work along with all the other peanut growers. It was my last chance and I went along with them. Frankly, I couldn't see how he was going to manage it, but what on Earth did I, an eleven-year-old girl, know about how men's minds work? Pascal not only quickly and efficiently completed all the tasks that my father assigned him, but also offered to do more difficult and exhausting ones. I heard him tell a young peanut grower that he had come here to build up his muscles and that the neighborhood kids would have trouble on their hands when he got back home. He demonstrated such vigor and aptitude that by mid-morning an argument broke out between two crews over which one got to have him. My father was bursting at the seams with pride. I heard him say to a coworker, not even caring if I overheard him, that he had always wanted a son like that.

And so the days passed and everything was turning out the reverse of what I had envisioned. At home, Pascal usurped my parents' love; in the streets, he only went up in my friends' admiration and respect and, as if that weren't enough, in the process his body turned toned and buff and he became gorgeous.

One day I found him on the riverbank talking with my group of friends. They no longer even bothered to send for me. He was teaching them Spanish. I joined the lesson in the capacity of instructor, correcting Ovida's pronunciation, and immediately Pascal disqualified me, saying that anyone incapable of pronouncing the word *perejil* without getting tongue-tied could not teach Spanish. They didn't even give me the chance to demonstrate to them that I could pronounce that word correctly. They split their sides with laughter. By some miracle I didn't burst into tears. Terrified at the possibility that Pascal would reduce me, in my very own village, to the misery characteristic of my visits to the city, I decided to break the promise I had made to Papa Vincent.

What can I tell you, *tifi*? I was desperate. None of my tactics had worked, but I still had a fourth phase to resort to, the summation of the first three.

4. *Ruination of the Soul.* In one fell swoop break his body, annul his position in the village and erase him forever from our family's memory. It was all too easy. Pascal himself had provided me with all the key elements. I would have to wait, that was true. My new position at the back of the line did not give me the right to suggest how we should invest our free time, but one fine day they accepted my proposal, which I'd made casually, without demonstrating too much interest, and we trampled back down the paths and swam in the swimming hole, and went once again to dry off in the sun on the top of the hill.

Pascal was an astute leader. He knew just how far he could push his inferiors and, remembering my friends' reaction the first time, he didn't dare repeat his idea—but that field, striped with red and yellow, called powerfully to him.

"I don't understand how a farm that no one works on can look so beautiful," he whispered to me.

"They work on it all the time," I said, "just not during the day."

"What?"

"The sun hurts their eyes."

Confused, Pascal tried a different angle.

"Why is the watchman who guards that village over on this side?" he whispered.

"Old Man Sadrak isn't guarding the cashew farmers," I replied. "He's guarding us."

"How's that?" asked Pascal. I was in total control.

"It seems unnecessary to me," I said, intentionally raising my voice. "The man hasn't been born who would dare cross that barbed wire."

His face hardened. He had perceived the challenge: I was calling his leadership into question. The rest had heard my words and stood up, scandalized. I had nothing to lose, and I ignored their admonishments.

"I'll bring you one right now," Pascal said, meaning a cashew fruit. "What color do you like?"

I pointed to the watchman's hut.

"That old man has instructions to shoot anyone who dares touch the fence, no matter who it is. To try to jump it now is stupid. You would come face to face with him, not with the cashew growers. But at night, Old Man Sadrak is drunk. . . ."

The rest of them had already retreated and were heading down the hill at a dead run, exempting themselves from having been even in the vicinity of that blasphemous conversation. Pascal started laughing.

"You're crazy," he said, believing that it would be enough to dismiss the challenge, not knowing that I, over the previous days, and thanks to him, had become an expert in masculine vices.

"I bet the neighborhood boys would be brave enough to do it," I said.

"What boys?" he asked. I stood up to leave.

"The ones who bashed your face in," I said.

■

It was close to midnight when we left. Earlier, I had greased the hinge on the door with soap so that it wouldn't make a sound. Papa Vincent was coughing more uncontrollably than ever; crouching down, we waited for him to stop. What would my parents have thought that my cousin and I were doing outside the house at that time of night if they had woken up? I didn't care.

There was a full moon in the sky. Fireflies in the scrub brush. The screech owls glided silently from one tree to another. The incessant clamor of insects surrounded us. I couldn't shake the feeling that someone was following us.

We came to the river, its gentle current painted silver in the moonlight, dammed up by turtles in heat; a formidable devil's drool trail. The hill. Old Man Sadrak's hut, snoring sounds, him no doubt stretched out on the floor, belly full of cane liquor. The grove. The village.

The cashews gleamed in the moonlight. A stripe of gold bordered by a stripe of ruby red. We approached the fence. Pascal prepared to jump over it. I stopped him.

"Red ones," I said, implacable. He jumped.

I lost sight of him almost at once, but I could still hear his footsteps for a while, ever farther off until I could no longer make them out. Satisfied, I turned halfway around to go back home to enjoy the sleep of the just when I saw, racing down the hill at a dead run, a small, black silhouette that blew past me like an exhalation and leaped over the fence in a single hop.

"Gracieusse!" I called in a loud voice, but not so loud as to awaken Old Man Sadrak. "Gracieusse!"

What can I tell you? I could live with my cousin's annihilation. But not with Gracieusse's. I jumped over too.

I lost count of how many times I peed on my dress. I couldn't see clearly where I was walking beneath the trees, in the dark, and the tears weren't helping matters. I had to find Gracieusse before the cashew growers started their worknight. The one I found was Pascal. He had his shirt filled with fruit.

"Piece of cake," he said.

"Shut up, you idiot," I told him. "We have to find Gracieusse."

"Gracieusse?"

"Drop that," I whispered with an intensity that surprised even me, at the same time that I gave his shirt a yank so that the stolen fruit would fall to the ground. "We don't have much time. Follow me."

We looked for her in vain all over that grove, calling out to her in hushed voices. My agitation and the intense reek of piss from my clothes gradually revealed to Pascal that we were in real and imminent danger. He started to get scared.

"Let's get out of here," he said. "She'll know how to get out."

"She came here to protect you," I told him. "You go back if you want to. I have to find her."

I had no other choice but to look for her in the village, and I started running towards it. When I came to the first houses I paused to catch my breath, and I realized that Pascal had not abandoned me. We dragged our feet for as long as we could until, marshaling our courage, we started running through the streets calling for Gracieusse. It was our terrible luck that at just that moment the cashew growers started coming out of their houses.

Out of all of the houses, all at the same time, as though obeying the summons of a whistle that only they could hear.

The main street was soon filled with men, women, and children dressed in rags, filthy and foul-smelling, their faces expressionless, their mouths open and their eyes blank, each one carrying the implements necessary for pruning their trees. I would have peed myself all over again, but there was nothing left in my bladder. Pascal did have enough, though, and let loose.

We had no choice but to abandon Gracieusse. I consoled myself with the thought that maybe she'd already escaped. We had to get out of there without being seen, and we started creeping back, plastered against the walls, crouching in the shadows, half dead with fright. After many failed attempts to slip away, we came to the village's storehouse. It was much larger than ours, and it was enveloped in the dense aroma of roasted nuts. The light from an oil lamp shone brightly from inside. Someone was crying. I stood on tiptoe and peeked through a window. The oil lamp was hanging from a beam and illuminated a veritable citadel of bundles stacked up to the roof. I confirmed what we all know but what no one dares to admit: the cashew growers were much more productive in their labors than we were in ours. In the center of the room, a table. At the table, a young man dressed in a black three-piece suit complete with a tie. A perfectly circular scar ringed his mouth. In his right hand, a jar of black sand. In front of him, two burly cashew growers held the disconsolate Gracieusse.

I called out to her, much to Pascal's horror. I couldn't help myself. She looked at us with bulging eyes and tried to free herself, but the well-dressed man stood up, pointed to us and said calmly: "Get them." We backed away, and only then did we realize that behind us were more than two hundred cashew growers, their eyes rolled back in their heads, advancing on us inexorably.

We took off like a shot toward the street, thinking that we could lose them—colossal stupidity, to try to confuse the locals. They came after us like bloodhounds on a scent. No matter where we went, there they were, right on our heels. More than once we came around a turn and ran straight into them. We were being pursued by several groups. Disheveled creatures, haggard peasants of cadaverous bearing, faces possessed of lightless eyes, besieged us from all sides. We got so lost among the narrow alleyways that we had no sense of where the grove was, our only escape route. Our desperation was such that we looked like guinea fowl running in circles—until Pascal, in a stab of recklessness, went inside one of the houses.

"No!" I screamed, and instantly bit my fist. We had doubled back behind a hut without being seen. My scream had alerted them, no doubt, and they would be coming at any moment. I had no alternative other than to enter the house as well.

I crouched down.

It smelled of dust, of dead leaves. It was dark. There were some bundles stacked here and there. A pair of rough-hewn

wooden chairs, overturned. Sitting at the table were two children, the father at the head. All of them staring into space with
extinct eyes. Mouths hanging open. Immobile.

Something hit me in the cheek and fell to the floor. A tender
cashew seed, black and curved, like a mummy's thumb. I turned
around and saw my cousin hiding behind the bundles. I joined
him, crawling across the cracked floorboards. I got a splinter.

"Are you crazy?"

Silence.

"Let's get out of here!" I told him in an intense whisper.

"Shut up," he said, and pointed to the diners. Toward them
(and toward us), through the ragged curtain that separated the
house from the backyard patio where the cookstove was, came a
disheveled sleepwalker with several steaming tin bowls in her
hands. Brusquely, she deposited them in front of her husband
and children and sat down herself.

And they started to eat.

The breakfast consisted of rocks, dirt, and hot manure.

Wracked by nausea, Pascal tried to crawl toward the door,
pulling on my clothes. The door stuck. Abandoning all caution,
we stood up and ran as fast as we could toward the patio. I tripped
over one of the children. I almost screamed. Shoving his way
through, Pascal yanked at the curtain and got tangled up in it.
He tore it to shreds trying to remove it from his face; it snarled
around his feet; he stomped on it. The family continued ingesting its meal of filth, unperturbed.

Outside, all was silent.

They've stopped chasing us, I thought, but at the same time I
knew that yes, they were still hunting us, that it was only a matter of time; because of a deceptively beneficial accident, we now
found ourselves at the intersection formed by communal back-
yards, apparently deserted, but only temporarily, a brief oasis
that would be rapidly occupied by the specters who had been

ordered to hunt us down and who would not give up on their task until carrying it out or receiving a counter-order. I was certain that our luck had run out. There was no escape.

We were quiet for a few seconds, deliberating over where to go. We didn't speak. In the darkness I could see Pascal's wide-open, bloodshot eyes begging for an answer.

And now, where to?

If I had had a few minutes to think and get oriented, I would have been able to take my cousin by the hand and head off in the correct direction, toward our village, beyond the cashew grove. But I was too afraid; I couldn't think, and my teeth wouldn't stop chattering. Even so, following a sudden impulse I began to move through the narrow yards. It was better to be moving in any direction at all than to stay grounded there, immobilized by fear, shipwrecked in a fraudulent calm, awaiting the consummation of a fate a thousand times worse than death. If our fate was already sealed, we would go to meet it on our own two feet, not await it paralyzed like lambs under the butcher's knife.

We moved along, taking advantage of the shadows' shadows, hopping from one hiding place to another; behind a barrel filled with water, behind an unhitched wagon tipped over on the rock-strewn road, behind boxes filled with rusted tools, behind a sleepy donkey tied to a solitary pile. At times we had to cross stretches of open space, running headlong, hunched over, nearly falling flat on our faces. And neither speed nor desperation prevented us from being fleeting witnesseses to images that would stay with us for the rest of our lives.

Sitting on the stoop of one house, wracked by an infernal cough, a man spitting colorful beetles that immediately dispersed in every direction.

A woman scrubbing clothes in a washbasin filled with mud.

A little girl petting a cat that she dropped when she saw us pass by. The animal fell to pieces on the ground; it was an old carcass.

An old man urinating dust on a barbed-wire fence. When he shook himself off, the head detached and got caught in the barbs. The old man buttoned up his pants and walked away as though nothing had happened. On the fence remained a part of his member, large, desiccated, and violet-colored, like a prune.

In a corral, several tireless hens, accompanied by their chicks, pecking at a human head surrounded by a cloud of flies.

A woman cutting her daughter's hair with a dull and rusty machete as though cutting weeds. The girl didn't bat an eye when her mother, accidentally, cut off her ear—or when she cut the other one off on purpose, to even things out.

A skeletal dog chewing and licking, licking and chewing a long bone—at the end of which was a shoe.

A feral pig the size of an old nag walking down an alleyway, rooting through the garbage. A boy sat astride its back, lighting the way with a torch—but it wasn't a torch. It was his hand ignited as a candle.

With each of these ephemeral visions I felt that I was leaving a not negligible part of my soul there on the trampled earth of that cursed village, but it was the last of them all that marked definitively the end of my childhood.

A very small boy held a string in his hands. The line trailed away from the boy and ascended. He was flying a kite. How many times had I been in that very same position, standing, my hands pulling and releasing in response to the resistance on the string, my face tilted toward the sky, in rapt contemplation of my kite dancing on the air. I had never flown a kite at night, obviously, but that macabre detail was not sufficient to prevent me from identifying with the boy, from feeling, suddenly, an uncontrollable tenderness—until my eyes, following the string, came to the kite: a used-up, rotted-out frame, consumed by the elements, trapped among the branches of a tree.

How long had it been there?

The answer to that question might have been enough to turn

my hair gray had I not tossed it aside to consider that the tree was a cashew. We were, miraculously, facing the grove. Pascal emitted a faint moan, but so urgent that I knew that it had not been the result of surprise or relief. I turned around. Behind us was a dense wall of cashew growers.

We took off at a dead run toward the grove with half of the village coming behind us.

I ran, my mind a blank. I ran without knowing where I was going. Without knowing if Pascal was still alongside me or not. I ran with my heart in my throat. The cashew growers also ran, but more agilely than us, making better decisions, as though they could see in the dark. Just before reaching the fence I sprained my ankle and fell. Prostrate on the ground, I saw how Pascal jumped over the fence and ran away up the hill—and how, when he realized that I had fallen behind, he came back for me. He picked me up off the ground and carried me, but it was too late. We were surrounded.

Oh, *tifi!* Your father's heart boomed in his chest like a kettle-drum. I hugged him and closed my eyes.

When nothing happened I opened them again and discovered that our pursuers were ignoring us, distracted by a faint glimmer that was coming toward us through the trees. We looked as well: it was a man ambling through the grove as though he had gone out for a walk. When he was close enough, we could see that the light with which he illuminated his steps did not come from a lamp but rather, emanated from his head. It was Papa Vincent, but not the hunched-over old man with the unsteady gait. How can I explain it to you, my girl? It was Papa Vincent in all his perfection. He stopped in front of the cashew growers, raised the index finger on his right hand, and moved it from side to side in a gesture that said "no." The cashew growers withdrew slowly. Papa Vincent approached us with a roguish smile. He rubbed my ankle and indicated with a signal that we should go. Pascal helped me to jump the fence, but my ankle no longer hurt. We flew back to the village.

Everyone was awake and crying bitterly. Papa Vincent had died, and they were keeping vigil over him in the storehouse. In the midst of the tumult my parents had not noticed our absence. Gracieusse's would go unremarked until well into the following day.

10. Spiral / Slippery Snake / Force of Habit

Mathilde looked straight ahead, glancing back only occasionally to make sure that I was following her without any problem, that no obstacles had sprung up between us. She led me to one of the side rooms. No matter how hard I looked for them, I couldn't see Isadore and Patricia Julia anywhere.

We entered a blue room infused with a different type of music. Mysteriously, the DJ's electronic din from the courtyard did not interfere with the eighties tunes that could be heard in here. Hanging from the ceiling were glass bubbles of different sizes that lit up in accordance with the vagaries of faint reflectors that changed colors. There were very few people in there. It was some sort of refectory, a place to rest, a lounge. On colorful sofas and armchairs, or reclined on cushions scattered at random over the floor, several couples sighed in each other's ears. In one corner I saw a spiral staircase ascend and pass through a small hole in the ceiling to the second floor. Against one wall was a bar attended by a lone bartender. Mathilde led me over to it and ordered two fantastical drinks that took the bartender a long time to prepare. As we waited, Mathilde, her elbow on the bar and her head resting on her hand, looked at me without speaking.

Our drinks served, Mathilde sipped from hers at length, motioning for me to do the same. I drank. . . . It was good. I leaned near to her, brought my lips to her ear, and, as I spoke, lightly brushed her earlobe; I could feel the metallic touch of her earring, but I could also hear the repercussion of my own breath, like an echo of mist that came back to me embellished by her perfume.

"Very good," I told her.

As I withdrew my mouth I could see that the skin on her neck had goosebumps, and when I resumed my position in front of her I saw her face aflame and her eyes open, extremely large, as though she were very angry. Inexplicably, she took my glass from my hand and deposited it next to hers on the bar. She took me by the hand and led me to the spiral staircase.

We began to climb. She went first. The staircase was really quite small and steep, so much so that if I fell behind, her calves would appear before my eyes, very close to my face; if I hurried up a bit, I almost brushed against her white thighs or the backs of her knees; and the one time that I tried to overtake her, my nose ran right into her backside.

She paused and looked at me over her shoulder. I had my nose practically buried in her shorts, growing intoxicated from a mixture of scents among which I could identify rose petal soap, apple-scented detergent, and another smell the origin of which eluded me, but which, added to the others, evoked in me a strange notion of cleanliness, of purity, of transparency.

Very slowly, lest I think that I should go back down and leave the way clear for her, she stepped backward onto the step immediately above mine. Now my eyes were level with her chin, but before settling there they traversed her neckline, noting how her skin seemed electrified at the place where her blouse, there where it covered her breasts, puffed noticeably out, incapable of hiding two sudden protuberances that vibrated as though emitting a desperate cry for help out into deep space. And when my eyes turned to hers, I saw that they were closed, and her open mouth sank down over my closed one like benevolent magma that first scorches and then nourishes and finally scorches all over again.

I was afraid.

I was afraid that she would find the pumice stone of my dead tongue, for which reason I kept my mouth closed. But her tongue was insistent and explored my lips for weak points, poorly sealed angles, like a slippery snake, until, having found a gap, it slid inside and, with a lever-like motion, parted the gates, opening them wide.

And to my surprise, my tongue, making contact with hers, became elastic and juicy and began to play a mollusks' fencing match with her tongue, with feints and blocks and surrenders. During one of my attacks I tasted once again the *look choop* that she'd pinched from me at the restaurant and, during one of hers, accents of the iced tea with ginger and rice whiskey that she'd drunk returned to me like an old memory. In a defensive move she revealed a specious flank that brought back to me the image of her *khao pad naem*, just exactly as I remembered it from when the waitress brought it to the table. And every time that she exhaled through her nose I tasted all over again the fantastic drink that we had abandoned on the bar.

I lost all notion of time. I recovered it when a very concrete humid sensation caused one of my cheeks to awaken as if from a dream. *My cheek*, I remember thinking. I opened my eyes, and was immediately overcome by the disquiet of not knowing when I had closed them. But I soon forgot all about that question because I observed that Mathilde was crying. She was crying silently. She was playfully nibbling at my lips while from her eyes tracks of tears plowed a crystalline furrow down her cheeks. *Her cheeks. My cheeks.* One of those jewels had fallen on my cheek. *On my cheek.*

Why was Mathilde crying? Had I hurt her? Was what we were doing too painful for her? Was it for me? What we were doing? Why was Mathilde crying? I obtained the shadow of an answer in an unusual way.

It is difficult to explain now, but if I strain my memory I can recall the words that I used in order to capture the moment that day. In fact, this entire chapter of my story is a literary recollection: the memory of the event itself grows fainter every day.

Suddenly I *imagined* that I was crying. For a magical instant *I was* Mathilde and *I knew* why she was crying. I could put myself in her place. I felt a tremendous shudder. I wasn't her, but I could be her, or rather, what was happening to her could have been happening to me. I was not her. I was not her. I was free of what was happening to her; she was something that responded to a situation that made her cry, and knowing this mysteriously demarcated limits that caused me to suspect that I, who was seeing her cry, was also something, something that was not her but that could think about her—a *being* on the receiving end of an experience who, although not crying himself, could somehow understand why the whole episode was making her cry—a sentient presence that was standing as witness to the miracle of her weeping.

Mathilde was crying from happiness.

And when I felt her happiness in myself, I felt like crying too. But then I got scared, because inside my body a strange person was stirring, a person who was trying to reap perceptions. An invader of sorts, though that invader was none other than myself. When I moved my face away and our lips went back to being our own, my eyes, just like hers, were overflowing. She raised her hand to her mouth to control her hiccups and her laughter, and with the same hand wiped her cheeks.

And me? I couldn't bear what was happening. The sensation was intolerable, worse than death, some sort of imminence. Of what? Not knowing made it unbearable. I moved away from Mathilde, whose face, at seeing me leave, changed from happiness to confusion and from confusion to agony.

My mental state, that strange sensation that had come over me, was precarious. I have used the word *imminence* in order to describe it, and my choice is not gratuitous. What I was feeling was something that hadn't yet fully manifested, been fulfilled. The suspense was terrible.

At the same time, or perhaps I should say for that same reason, to remain under the strange conditions I've described required a high degree of concentration. I knew that, were I to lose focus for even a few seconds, it would be enough for everything to vanish, like the images from a dream, like certain intuitions, like any epiphany. What was happening to me, this new perspective that was invading me, was slow to establish itself, but I also felt that to leave it suspended in the air *until* it concretized would have been more difficult than balancing a pin on a silk thread. Being face to face with Mathilde, however, seeing her, was helping me, and that is why I fled.

I was too accustomed to death not to be terrified by these new developments.

Ghost in the Shell

Our senses report having been stimulated to a centripetal presence that we know as the "self." Amazingly, this presence (resulting from the neural activity of the brain's frontal lobe) is aware of its own existence and does not identify with the existence of the body (ignorant of itself). This gap engenders in the self the sensation of being separate from the body, inside of which it dwells as a prisoner: the classic "ghost in the shell" effect.

The punctuality with which the self receives reports of the most minuscule of stimuli causes it to believe that it has dominion over the body and that it plays a leading role in the saga of survival. It does not understand that the body, motivated by automatic processes generated in the brain (which is the same as saying, generated by itself), makes multitudes of vital decisions every day and every hour without consulting it. This is why one of the principal functions of the self is to overvalue itself.

The self generates an acknowledgement of receipt every time it receives the report of a stimulus. This acknowledgement of receipt is called emotion. There exist innumerable emotions—as many as there are stimuli. Nevertheless, we human beings invest all of our time and energy in steering our senses toward the pursuit of stimuli that always produce one emotion in particular: happiness.

Many authors and philosophers more qualified and learned than I have tried to define the emotion that we know as happiness. The majority of them have declared the task impossible, given that happiness differs according to each person's criteria; for some, happiness is one thing, while for others it is something else, at times completely contrary. The difficulty arises from a simple error: they confuse the emotion with the stimulus. They try to define happiness by utilizing, as raw material, the stimuli that each person needs in order to induce it. Of course, they fail.

What is certain is that happiness is the same emotion for every person.

Independent from what each individual needs to achieve it, once it is achieved we all experience a sensation of supreme well-being. But this sensation of supreme well-being, like the color red, is nothing more than an invented word. That word designates a state of absolute equilibrium: we do not lack for anything, desire is eradicated, the self is silent, disappears, and we emerge into the imperturbable void, the glorious stillness of nothingness. But, like all things in equilibrium, this precarious balance is easily lost, and, upon losing it, the self returns more conceited than ever, desire is exacerbated, the cycle repeats itself, and we're impelled to resume the search over and over again.

At great advantage are those who need only simple stimuli to induce happiness. Unfortunate are those who can find it only through complicated stimuli and through the investment of excessive amounts of energy. We avoid unhappiness, that diabolical emotion, because it reaffirms the self. Happiness erases it.

Our home is the void.

Ironically, the self constantly seeks its own annihilation.

11. PARSIMONY

I left the lounge and plunged back into the crowd in the interior courtyard. I did not feel afraid. Everything had already been erased. I wanted to leave, and I would have done so had Patricia Julia not grabbed me firmly by the hand (I thought that my phalanges would turn to dust beneath her talons) and taken me away from the tumult.

Once again I allowed myself to be led. I guessed that Patricia Julia was taking me to a less crowded place; once there, I would orient myself better in order to find the exit and I would say goodbye; I would give some excuse and would not allow myself to be persuaded otherwise. It did not happen like that.

Patricia Julia dragged me all the way to the other side of the huge dance floor, toward the lounges on the other side. It was useless to protest. The lounge that we entered on this side was larger, dimly lit, and decorated in red tulle that hung from the ceiling in a capricious configuration. The result was a sort of hazy, blurry labyrinth. The music was a dreamlike fusion of sitars, oboes, and electronic guitar that sounded like the full-bodied soundtrack to a movie filmed in exotic locales with futuristic props—a spice route through intergalactic space.

Instead of sofas and armchairs, there were Moroccan divans of different sizes dispersed along the length and width of that space, surrounded by thick red and pink candles. Reclining peacefully upon the cushions, scarcely distinguishable in the candlelight, various couples talked or embraced; two and even three couples shared the largest of them. With me by the hand, which she was grasping tightly, as though she feared I would get away from her, Patricia Julia swiftly evaluated the availability of the divans. They were all occupied. Without wasting any time, she dragged me toward the spiral staircase, and we went up to the second floor, where the same configuration we'd seen on the first floor was repeated. Except on this floor there was a vacant divan—toward which another couple, closer to it than we were, was moving. We would never make it in time, and Patricia Julia knew it. She released my hand and went off alone.

I cannot relate what happened next with complete fidelity because the distance did not allow me to hear precisely the words that were exchanged. What's certain is that Patricia Julia went up to the couple, who had already settled onto the cushion, and lay down next to them. The man was left speechless. The girl looked at the man, begging for an explanation. Patricia Julia looked at them defiantly. I thought I heard her say (or perhaps I only read her lips): "What are you waiting for?" as she patted the cushion. The girl took off in a panic. The man, slowly, and without taking his eyes off of Patricia Julia, followed her. Then Patricia Julia fixed her eyes on me and ordered me to come to her with a single crook of her index finger. I went. Patricia Julia received me and drew the veil around us.

She took off her high heels and took off my shoes. After placing them underneath the divan, she took off my jacket. She wanted us to be comfortable. She took my head between her hands and lay me back on a cushion. I was stretched out on my back. She did not take her eyes off mine, not even when she lay down next to me, on her side, her body turned toward mine. We stayed like that for a few moments until, gathering her courage, Patricia Julia drew me to her with one hand and, aided by her right leg, which went across my waist and wound underneath my thigh, she pressed against me, squeezing me, and rendering me helpless, in an incontestable wrestler's hold.

After nibbling on my earlobe, she introduced her tongue into my ear, and I, who had been rather careless with my sepulchral "hygiene" in the past few days, crossed my fingers that a centipede wouldn't slide into her mouth. That she didn't scream suddenly and run away in terror let me know that we were safe from that possibility.

I was worried about the pressure of her right knee on my lower belly and any other parts that she could accidently crush. I brought my hand near her thigh, that immaculate anaconda, in order to move it, not knowing that to touch it would unleash a curse worse than death. Because her skirt was a poor excuse, a refutable argument, a timid opinion, a cloth hesitation, a technicality, my repugnant zombie hand, sent to combat the invulnerable, came in direct contact with her flesh, oh inexpressible substance, protected by a nefarious halo of lethal toxins that plunged me once again into the dangerous neurosis from which I had so recently fled.

Having thought about it a great deal in the solace of my house during the days following the events, I think that the best way to explain what happened is by saying that the action that I initiated, on the surface simple and opportune, ran into a series of absurd and insurmountable difficulties.

The first was the almost immediate refusal of my hand to use its strength to lift my friend's thigh from the first moment that it touched it. At first I marveled at this total abdication, because it seemed to be a private matter of my hand, a unilateral decision, although gradually I realized that I had been, and continued to be, an accomplice to that renunciation. The reason, as I understand it, had to do with the unexpected springing to life of my sense of touch and its subsequent overload and collapse, which occurred simultaneously. For the first time, my sense of touch was telling me something about myself, once again obliging me to listen to a story that defined me as the recipient of a fundamental experience that, in this case, focused on what I can only describe as an inconceivable softness.

My fingers, my fingertips, the palm of my hand felt this impossible softness but also the resistance and firmness of the muscles that it concealed, and in my hand a desire awoke, consistent with my own, to verify if that softness and firmness were in evidence along the entire length of the leg or if they were localized qualities restricted to that part upon which my hand had happened to alight. As a consequence, I did not manage to carry out my initial goal of getting her leg off of me, but rather ended up settling it more firmly on top of me in order to carry out my explorations more comfortably.

I slid my hand down along the anterior side of her leg and confirmed that it was equally soft along its entire length: a marvel of smoothness highlighted, not interrupted, by the bony hardness of knee and shin, cunningly and perfectly concealed beneath the sleek surface of her golden skin. It was a brief acknowledgement, a preparatory exercise, an outbound trip without layovers, of a purely instructive nature. . . . The return voyage along the back side of her leg—now that truly did constitute an epic poem worthy of being sculpted in marble as the pride of future generations of zombies.

As it happened, upon reaching the ankle, my hand rotated and cupped the heel like a stirrup, and even the heel was soft and defenseless: I could not have chosen a better port of departure. My hand began the ascent with a certain timidity, as though foreseeing events of great significance for which it wasn't prepared. Or no, perhaps it wasn't timidity but rather that maddening meticulousness of the traveler who doesn't want to miss a single detail of the panoramas offered up by the regions he is visiting. The most likely is that both are necessary to explain the parsimony with which my hand ascended Patricia Julia's leg.

From the heel I moved on to the ankle, but this time from behind, and its slenderness made me close my hand. My hand rose without changing position, opening only as much as necessary to span the curve of calf, magic island, oasis of delights, immortal dune, sugared crumpet, torch of all fires, repository of liquid metals, cosmic oval around which the entire universe rotates.

Halfway up the calf my hand refused to continue, intrigued by two new sensations that complicated the already complex concept of softness: malleability and turgidity. But I insisted. I insisted, and it was only thanks to this enormous force of will that I managed to prevent my hand from remaining forever beached on her calf, kneading and palpating it as though trying, though unsuccessfully, to detect falsehoods, errors, or treasures inside it—as though chewing on it.

And without giving up this motion of systole and diastole, that of a convulsing spider or of an octopus too wise for its own good, a claw that strangles and releases, strangles and releases, adopting it as the best way to advance upon that sweet and treacherous terrain, my hand, after a brief respite in the hollow of the knee to gather strength, set off on the adventure of the thigh, that interminable steppe, in the direction of the unknown.

My hand spent hundreds of years on her thigh, thousands of years, millions of years, but hand years, not human years, so brief, and in that incalculable time it acquired new experiences and learned new techniques in order to progress on its journey, pinching, sliding, caressing with the palm, caressing with the wrist, squeezing, applying pressure, tickling, and always, always, always, always moving upwards. *I* was directing it. I, I, I. My hand was my bathyscaphe, my lunar pod, the probe that *I* had sent out to collect vital information, to extract the secrets of softness. And lo and behold, after eons, my hand came across an elevation without handholds, a mound, a round vault that fascinated and stupefied it all at once. I don't know how long it idled indecisively in the foothills of her buttocks, but when at last it embarked upon the ascent it learned that the accumulation of all that had occurred up until that point had been a precise training exercise in anticipation of this moment in which all of the experiences from the journey were justified and in which all that had been learned would be put into practice.

I took possession of that roundness as pure and generous as a field in springtime, tremulous and succulent flesh, deceptively malleable, upon which an open hand, any open hand, *my* open hand, recovered remnants from an ancestral memory having to do with the orb of light from which all things originate.

With a spiral movement that eventually encompassed the other buttock, I pressed, weighed, and squeezed, climbing up to the waist, so narrow, so ephemeral, so precarious that isthmus from which hung the masses that my hand was ravaging, fruit far too heavy for such a fragile leafstalk, fruit arcing towards earth. And I remembered that all vaults harbor gods, treasure arks guarded by whimsical beings, and a colossal greed awoke in me, and I lifted the fine strip, the taut cord, the silk thread, the Sol string, the delicate filament, the iridescent elastic that bound her underwear to her body, and I plunged my hand into the depths of the headland that divided her buttocks, which, feeling that sacrilegious intrusion, contracted, catching me, trapping me, immobilizing me.

Caught between Scylla and Charybdis, I could scarcely move the tips of my fingers, but I wormed them in and soon managed to awake in Patricia Julia a curious fragility infiltrated by fear. Up until that moment she hadn't ceased licking my ear, nibbling and sucking, boldly venturing to my throat, the nape of my neck. Now she had suddenly stopped, frozen in anticipation, as though she wanted to concentrate better on what was about to happen to her and couldn't do it if she were otherwise occupied. Apprehensive, but intrigued, she relaxed her buttocks, giving me the space that I needed in order to maneuver. Not losing any time, having gained the cooperation of her buttocks, I sought and found her anus, illustrious ring, and, when I touched it, an image of a distant galaxy formed before my inner eye. Tender, soft, brimming with health, the most beautiful of wedding rings, when my caresses became more expressive, it turned suddenly hard, stiff, furrowed, a lightning-quick movement that reminded me of the hunting tactics of certain carnivorous plants. Patricia Julia remained motionless, frozen, as though the behavior of her surly anus were at the outer edges of her responsibility. And so it was I who had to calm it with sweet caresses, make it promises of kindness, pamper and soothe it until it turned back into a wrinkled, soft little mass, hungry for my fingers. I introduced my index finger up to the first joint and Patricia Julia arched her back to swallow the finger up to the second as she brought her face near to mine and bit me on the cheek. I felt the pain and responded by sliding my finger in up to the knuckle. Then, letting out a long moan of pleasure, Patricia Julia contracted the pristine muscle around my finger, grasping it with an uncommon strength, like a winch, and then suddenly seized the rest of my hand between her buttocks, perfect mandibles, with an even greater strength.

The hunter had been hunted.

Submerged in an unbreakable trance and moaning continually, Patricia Julia began to chew my finger by rapidly relaxing and contracting her anus, a pulsing parody of the digestive process. My index finger was consumed little by little, but as it slowly disappeared from my hand, it slowly reappeared as if by magic between my legs. I screamed.

Terrified, I stood up on the divan, hitting my head on the frame of the netting. I started to retreat as I simultaneously and chaotically straightened my shirt, put on my jacket, looked for my shoes, and smoothed my pants. I reached the edge and I fell, tangled up by the dense netting that had just barely concealed our intimacy. On my back on the floor, ensnared and diminished, I could see Patricia Julia on her knees on the cushion, adjusting her skirt and looking all around her, howling with laughter. I emerged from my net with great difficulty, and once free, I ran.

When at last I plunged once again into the crowd, I was completely back to normal.

La Citadelle

They say that the Tontons Macoutes trapped my grandfather Vincent as he was sailing for the Isle à Vaches hidden beneath a canvas on a small fishing boat. Papa Doc, who was afraid of him, ordered him not to be killed, as it would have been a serious tactical error to confer upon such a formidable opponent the advantage of being sent to the Other Side. Better to take him prisoner, and so he was locked up, in chains, in the deepest cell of the Citadelle.

As the villagers tell it, the most prestigious and dangerous dissident witch doctors from the region were imprisoned in the Citadelle. Accordingly, the secret penitentiary was governed by a battery of important sorcerers friendly to the regime. They say that the authorities had siphoned off the most corrupt and demonic from the ranks of the Tontons Macoutes to man the garrison. According to Papa Vincent, some of the jailers were demons incarnated as ordinary civilians, tortured souls that had returned thirsty for revenge and even beings from the depths sent to this world by mistake. Others were zombies. In other words, they were people immune to magic. What they hadn't counted on was the fact that the Devil is wise because he's old, not because he's the Devil, and that my great-grandfather was an ace at discerning situations that required his talent for magic and those that called for his aptitude for a good swindle.

The other sorcerers in the cell with Papa Vincent had lost eyes, tongues, and ears to torture, all except a young man named Placide, a recent arrival like himself.

They had read their destiny clearly in the wounds and mutilations of the others. They knew that soon enough they, too, would suffer the punishment reserved for those who refused to ·

use their powers against the enemies of the dictator. No one else would speak to them or look at them or listen to them, and so the two became friends and set about thinking on how they might escape. They didn't have to think very hard to conclude that the only way they could leave the Citadelle was as dead men. And so they set to work.

They didn't have time to wait for one of their cellmates to die in order to employ the classical and literary appropriation of his shroud. In any case, it would have been necessary for two of them to die, not just one. Neither Papa Vincent nor Placide felt particularly disposed toward accelerating the end for one of those poor earless wretches. Thus, they would have to simulate their own deaths.

For a talented witch doctor this was no great feat. To fall into a trance and suspend vital functions for an hour or two was an entirely routine task. The problem was that the jailers would not be the least bit impressed by a body lying inert for a few hours. The day that both were brought to the Citadelle, the guards removed from the cell that they now occupied the body of a man who'd been dead for seven days. They dressed him in a black three-piece suit, white shirt, tie, and patent leather shoes—a final tribute or the last jest from Papa Doc to his adversaries.

Placide was a novice, and Papa Vincent was worried that they'd be found out because of him. He spoke to him. He reminded him that he should not come out of his hibernation for anything in the world until he told him to. It wasn't simply a matter of remaining motionless for the period of time necessary to trick the jailers, but rather, also long enough to face whatever dangers might arise once they were taken out. Neither of the two knew for certain what the Tontons Macoutes did with those dead men dressed in their party clothes. Placide, who was an optimist, handsome and good-natured, gave him his word.

Since Papa Vincent told his stories one time and one time only, and would not repeat them no matter how much one begged, those who had the privilege of hearing this one will have to resort to their own memories of that singular occasion in order to confirm how many days Papa Vincent and Placide played dead. Of course, there are discrepancies. Some say it was three days; others, three weeks. Some say it was a month. What they do agree on is that, one day, the two friends awoke foaming at the mouth. The idea was to make the guards believe that they had killed themselves by swallowing some kind of poison.

For days, the number of which is not worth specifying, they lay in the same position without moving a muscle. Neither gave in to the temptation of comfort. They didn't eat, they didn't drink. They scarcely breathed. Their cellmates were the first to be fooled, and they grumbled to get the guards' attention. At the end of however long it was the guards came in, dressed them, and took them away. In the rarefied atmosphere of the jail, in which the pestilence of rotten meat mixed with the fragrance of accumulated feces, no one noticed the strong smell of living sweat that floated about the two "dead men."

They lay them out on the ground. Papa Vincent was afraid that they would burn them or bury them in a common grave and so was quite surprised when, after an hour's journey, the guards tossed them onto the grass and left at a trot. Papa Vincent wasn't ready to cry victory. Something was wrong. It couldn't be that easy. He was worried that Placide, carried away by impetuousness, would get up, but, just as the young man had promised, he didn't do it. Then Papa Vincent opened his eyes, just a slit, and through a chink in his eyelashes saw two devils dressed in black three-piece suits, white shirts, and ties approaching: they were Typhus and Macluclús.

"Look, Macluclús, more new suits," said Typhus.

"That kind of suit," said the obese Macluclús, kicking Papa Vincent, "could look really good on Famine."

"What a party!" exclaimed Typhus. "Almost all of us are dressed already!"

They began to undress them: Macluclús undressed Papa Vincent, and Typhus undressed Placide. Typhus said:

"Macluclús, I am so unlucky. This guy stinks too much. It's making me queasy."

"What does he smell like?" asked Macluclús

"I have never been so close to a dead man who stank so badly. He smells like viscera from the catacombs smoked over cow dung!"

Macluclús started laughing. Papa Vincent realized that they were enjoying themselves. But a devil's fun is always a trick, and he prepared himself for the worst. Macluclús had already gotten his jacket off. Typhus had not managed to do the same with Placide.

"Macluclús," said Typhus, pinching his nose between his fingers, "I can't stand it, I swear to you."

"Does he smell that bad?"

"As if a sick cat had emptied his bowels on top of a pig carcass and then covered his excrement in brimstone!"

Macluclús, doubled over with laughter, had moved on to unknotting Papa Vincent's tie; he'd already taken off his vest.

Typhus, for his part, gave a start every time he tried to take off Placide's jacket.

"Macluclús, help!" he shouted.

"What does it stink like, Typhus, what does it stink like?"

"Like a Cyclops's scrotum!" cried Typhus. "Like a rhinoceros's earwax! Like a leper's pustules! The breath of a lion who ate a pigmy with the pox couldn't beat this one's stench!"

Macluclús laughed and laughed. Through the chink in his eyelashes, Papa Vincent noticed that Placide's lower lip was trembling. He began to despair.

And so things continued, Macluclús undressing Papa Vincent and Typhus making Macluclús laugh with his nonsensical similes without having managed to remove the first article of Placide's clothing.

Macluclús had finished removing Papa Vincent's socks and shoes, leaving him completely naked on the grass, when Typhus, pulling away once again from Placide, announced: "Macluclús, this dead guy reeks so badly that it is our duty to take him and burn him in one of hell's ovens. It's the least we can do."

Placide couldn't bear it any longer. He opened his eyes, stood up, and shouted: "I'm not dead!"

But then, with a lightning-quick motion, Typhus covered Placide's mouth with a glass jar that slowly began filling up with a red vapor. Placide kicked his feet, but the lean and gnarled Typhus only pressed the jar harder over his mouth until Placide closed his eyes again and fainted. Typhus withdrew the jar and screwed on a lid.

"Got you!" he said.

"Typhus" admonished Macluclús, "we only have permission to take their clothing. Nothing more."

"Ah!" said Typhus. "What an obedient little boy! Would you feel better if I left him something in exchange?"

"Yes, in fact," replied Macluclús.

"Very well," said Typhus, searching his pockets. "Let's see. . . . Here! What do you think? One cashew seed and one peanut. You can't deny that I'm a spendthrift."

"Typhus . . . ," warned Macluclús.

"All right, all right," said Typhus. "Let's see what else I have. . . . Perfect! My recipe for the preparation of black sand. What do you think? It will make him rich!"

"Not bad," said Macluclús, "but I know just the thing. Leave him a little bit of your white sand so that he can cure himself one day, if he wants to, from what you did to him today."

"Macluclús!" whined Typhus.

"Then give him back what you took from him. I don't want trouble with the boss because of you."

Typhus thought it over. After a few moments he took a little transparent bottle filled with white sand from the inside pocket of his jacket and left it next to Placide.

"Happy?" asked Typhus.

"Yes," said Macluclús.

"Let's go, then," said Typhus, and they left.

When he judged it opportune, Papa Vincent stood up and went to help Placide, who came to with great difficulty and displayed a circle of blood around his mouth.

And so, one of them naked and the other one dressed, they walked away from that place.

And Papa Vincent noticed that Placide was no longer optimistic or good-natured or handsome.

After a great deal of walking, they came to a valley through which ran a crystalline river, and they decided to stay there. But Papa Vincent wanted to plant peanuts, alleging that the cashew is a malevolent plant that causes welts, and Placide wanted to plant cashews, alleging that the peanut drew a very low market price. Papa Vincent said that there were more important things than money. Placide responded that no one had ever been able to demonstrate to him, with concrete evidence, that this was true. And as they could not reach an agreement, they divided up the infernal gifts: Placide kept the recipe and Papa Vincent the sand, not to mention that each kept a seed from the supernatural stock with which they would found their respective villages on opposite sides of the river. They never spoke to one another again.

12. The Fleeting Miracle / The Obstinacy of Ignorance

"I don't know exactly when I put my shoes back on."

"Which is to say that when you left there you were barefoot," concluded Dionisio.

"I went down the stairs carrying them in my hands. I was completely disheveled, with my shirttails hanging out. My belt buckle was undone; I don't understand why. I didn't finish putting myself together before I ran off. I must have put my shoes back on when I went downstairs, sitting on the bottom steps. . . . Well, but, what could that small detail possibly matter?"

"Just trying to help," said Dionisio. "I'm looking for clues."

"Clues."

"Clues, yes. Indications. I want to help you to understand what happened—and in doing so, understand it myself. I would like to reconstruct the scene in all of its details. What harm can come to us from trying to understand everything, if we can?"

"Very well," I said, contrite, although not entirely convinced of his argument. "I'm sorry."

"It's all right," said Dionisio. "You were in a state of total disarray, barefoot, running the risk of being run through by a poisoned blade, placed there on purpose right where they knew you'd be walking. Poisons can't kill you, but they can certainly have other types of effects, all of them unpredictable."

"I see," I acknowledged. "But no, I don't remember stepping on any traps."

"You wouldn't have realized it if you had."

"Why do you say that?"

"Because you were in an altered state, confused, by your own admission. A bear trap could have bitten you and taken off your entire foot and you wouldn't have noticed until you'd gotten home."

"Possibly," I admitted.

"Additionally," continued Dionisio, "you had been drinking."

"Can alcohol intoxicate the dead?"

"The consensus is no," replied Dionisio. "However, allow me to ask you a question: Would we realize it if we were drunk?"

It was a good question.

"Look around you," said Dionisio, making a gesture with his head intended to encompass the whole place in one sweep: zombies chatting over drinks. "Why do they do it unless it has the same effect on them as on the living? Because of its astringent qualities? Are we really going to swallow that story?"

"It's a good point," I said, a bit embarrassed.

"In any case," said Dionisio, ignoring my concession, "alcohol isn't the only thing we have to worry about."

"I don't understand."

"Have you forgotten, perchance, that you had also eaten a late dinner, and worse, with exotic ingredients? Foodstuffs from other latitudes, heavily spiced?"

"I hadn't really taken that into account."

"I am certain that all of these things, combined in specific proportions, were the causes of your ordeal."

"Ordeal? I wouldn't call it an ordeal. . . ."

"Call it what you like," said Dionisio impatiently. "Don't change the subject."

"That is the subject."

"No. The subject is not the mental chaos in which you found yourself enveloped, but rather the chain of events that served to detonate it."

"But Dionisio," I implored, "don't you realize that this chaos of which you speak could be . . ."

"Of course I realize it," said Dionisio, "but since it would be impossible for us to be sure, it's best to just forget about it. Already all you can do is remember the words that occurred to you at that moment in order to describe the situation. Today they are nothing more than empty words, husks."

"I couldn't have told you about it in any other way."

"And I thank you for it. But you have to admit that instead of making things easier, the irrational way in which you chose to tell me what happened. . . ."

"I know."

"And so what? Let's just call it a strange symptom of your temporary loss of composure and leave it at that."

"Okay."

We were silent for a few moments.

"Now what?" I asked, despairing.

"What I told you," reiterated Dionisio. "The most advantageous thing for us to do now is to focus on the details, on the mechanical aspect of the question; things that could have happened to you without your noticing, recounted precisely, insofar as possible. I am not interested in hearing the details of the madness that came over you, much less narrated with the words that this same madness provided you, a madness which, if I'm not mistaken, reaches its apogee with the third girl."

"That's right."

"After all's said and done, you already experienced it. No matter how hard you try, you will never manage to make me understand, and you yourself have already gone back to being immune to it, regardless of how tightly you cling to the words that it generated."

"You're right."

"And isn't it your desire, to make a long story short, to re-create the conditions that would permit you to reproduce that mysterious delirium?"

"It is."

"Well, then, it would behoove you to focus and to tell me as clearly as possible everything that you remember."

"I'm ready."

"Very good," said Dionisio. "You fled from Patricia Julia in an absolute panic, your clothing rumpled, barefoot. You went down the spiral staircase and you paused on the landing to put on your shoes. . . ."

"It was a spiral staircase," I interrupted, "it didn't have a landing."

"Fine then," said Dionisio with a touch of impatience. "It didn't have a landing."

"I thought that every detail was important," I explained.

"Okay," he said. "And so, what happened?"

"I ran."

"To where?"

"I wanted to leave. I wanted to find the exit. But no matter where I might have wanted to go, I would have to cross the dance floor."

"I understand. You crossed the dance floor."

"With great difficulty. Everybody was dancing frenetically; either they were in no mood to let me pass by, or they simply did not notice my presence."

"You advanced slowly."

"Very slowly."

"Did you run into anyone you knew along the way?"

"No one."

"Did anyone touch you?"

"Everybody touched me! It was impossible for them not to!"

"I mean in a special way, intentionally."

"No. No one."

"What did you do after that?"

"When I had almost made it to the other side, I remembered that that was where I had left Mathilde, and I changed course."

"Where did you go?"

"It was a stupid move. Obviously, Mathilde would have already gone off somewhere else. Why would she have stayed in the same place that entire time?"

"That's reasonable."

"But I didn't think about it like that. I wanted to avoid running into her."

"And so you had Patricia Julia behind you and Mathilde in front of you, or so you believed. Two routes were left for you to choose from."

"Really only one, because one side was occupied by the bar and the DJ platform."

"True."

"I moved toward the arched hallway."

"Encountering the same difficulties, I'd imagine."

"Yes. But I shoved my way through."

"I see."

"In such a way that as I walked I left a trail of irritated people behind me."

"To be expected."

"I didn't stop until I'd reached the foyer. I was one step from the exit . . ."

"And what happened?"

"I saw Isadore."

"Did she wave to you? Did she call out your name?"

"Neither one."

"And so?"

"I had passed by in front of her, but she didn't even see me. She was talking with several men."

"Hmmm. . . ."

"I was one step from the exit. . . . The archways were not as crowded as they had been a few hours earlier. I could have left easily."

"You could have left . . . but you didn't leave?"

"I didn't leave."

"What made you change your mind?"

"I thought that we agreed not to discuss that topic."

"And you are not mistaken. Excuse my lapse. Continue."

"I approached her. The scene was very . . . uncomfortable, seeing her talking to those men."

"I don't understand why, but it doesn't matter; don't even think about explaining it to me. Don't get held up."

"I approached her slowly so as to give her time to spot me, but at the same time I wanted to hide, and so I wouldn't be so obvious, I approached from the side."

"You suddenly felt a qualm about being too 'obvious.' . . ."

"Yes."

"You wanted her to see you coming, but you also wanted her to think that you were arriving in a casual, accidental way."

"Exactly."

"Why?"

I shrugged my shoulders.

"Forget I said anything. . . . Go ahead. Did it happen the way you wanted it to?"

"Not at all."

"I'm listening."

"Well, as I've already told you, I approached her slowly . . ."

"To surprise her."

"Partly."

"Go on; and?"

"When I got close enough, and since, to be heard, the men really had to raise their voices, I heard what they were saying."

"What were they saying?"

"Nonsense. The typical stupid things that people say in order to keep the conversation lively and to get to know one another."

"But . . ."

"But, as I was listening to them, I realized several things."

"Like what?"

"Well, in the first place, there were three of them."

"Very good. Three individuals, three males."

"But only one of them was really interested in talking to Isadore."

"And the other two?"

"The other two were surely there to offer him emotional support. They intervened to laugh at his jokes; if they said anything, it was to reiterate something that their leader had said."

"And Isadore?"

"Isadore was all charm."

"Was he someone she knew, perhaps?"

"He was not."

"And what else happened?"

"Everything happens now. Pay attention."

"Whenever you're ready."

"I was already practically next to her when I heard that the man was insisting that Isadore go and dance with him."

"And did Isadore accept?"

"No, Isadore did not accept."

"I understand."

"And now it really was impossible for her not to see me."

"But she ignored you. She acted as though she didn't see you."

"That's what I thought."

"Were you mistaken?"

"I believe so."

"Why?"

"Because of what happened after."

"Do tell."

"The man was insisting. He said that he wouldn't take no for an answer. The phrase rubbed me the wrong way. It was aggressive. Up until that point the exchange had been friendly, light, and suddenly, with that ultimatum, it transformed into something different, risky, and, to a certain extent, offensive."

"How did Isadore react?"

"As if nothing were happening. She didn't alter her smile, she didn't furrow her brow, she didn't demonstrate any sign of annoyance. But she replied, looking him straight in the eye, that she didn't want to dance with him, and that short of dragging her onto the dance floor by force, she didn't see any way that he would attain his goal."

"And did he drag her by force?"

"Of course not!"

"What happened next?"

"Something surprising."

"Tell me."

"She said that, in any case, she was there with her boyfriend, and if she ever felt like dancing she would do so with him and no one else. Then she reached out and took my hand, interlacing her fingers with mine. Without looking, Dionisio, without looking. Somehow she knew my location, had known the entire time, had seen me without my realizing it and had calculated my trajectory. She had been focusing her attention on my approach, even while she was talking to the three men."

"She took your hand?"

"To make them believe that I was her boyfriend."

"Okay, okay . . . ," said Dionisio, and then paused a long while ruminating over a thought. "With what objective?"

"So that they would go away!"

"Of course!" said Dionisio. "Of course, obviously. And did they?"

"At first they appeared confused, given that they had seen me arrive and had judged me just another person, someone passing by, trying to clear a path in the crowded nightclub. Then they moved from confusion to surprise and from surprise to embarrassment."

"What did you do?"

"I stood next to Isadore, I played my part. The man who had

asked her to dance apologized to us and went away. The other two had already moved away, embarrassed, under the pretext that someone was calling to them."

"Okay. . . . They didn't tell you their names?"

"What? Their . . . ? No, they didn't tell me their names."

"It would have been a good excuse to shake your hand and inject some kind of substance into it."

"Dionisio, by God," I said, exasperated. "And how then would you explain the two incidents that occurred before that? No one had injected me with anything and just look at what happened to me!"

"Was it the first time that you had seen them, these men?"

"But what does that . . . ? Yes!"

"Hmmm. . . . Are you sure?"

"Very sure."

"How can you be sure? You yourself said that there was a throng of people, chaos."

"You're right," I admitted. "Let's put it this way: as far as I know, that was the first contact that I'd had with them."

"Better. Better," repeated Dionisio, satisfied. "So then they went away and you and Isadore were left alone. What happened then?"

Before answering, I leaned across the bar and grasped him by the shoulder.

"I came back to life, Dionisio. I came back to life."

"Though I know full well that it will not lead to anything," said Dionisio, defeated, "explain yourself."

I took a few seconds to put my thoughts in order before speaking. I wasn't sure where to start. Whereas, from the point of view of a casual witness, what occurred might appear trivial and ordinary, for me it was just the opposite: a mystical, unrepeatable, and practically indescribable experience. Externally, nothing important had happened; inside me, however, something marvelous and fundamental had occurred, after which nothing would ever be the same again. I decided that the best approach was to simplify my narration to the maximum extent. It was very likely that I wouldn't succeed.

"Well . . . ," I said. "The men went away and were soon lost in the crowd, forgotten and indistinguishable. Isadore and I, however, remained with our hands intertwined. It was as if neither one of us wanted to make the decision to let go, but there was also something else, a strange sensation that we had lost our hands forever, that our hands, from that moment forward, could not exist unless they were intertwined."

"How do you know that she thought the same thing?"

"I don't know if she thought the same thing. Not with absolute certainty."

"But you speak as if, in fact, you knew what she was thinking, as if you had thought and felt the same thing."

"At that moment I couldn't think of any other explanation for her reluctance to let go of my hand."

"That's fair."

"But it was something immediate, do you understand? I only realized that she had taken my hand when I looked and verified it by sight. Before I had felt only a strange current, a soft electricity, uncomfortable and pleasant all at once. Have you seen those radio telescope photos from deep space? Images of galaxies whose tentacles of light spin around a dazzling nucleus of indescribable energy? Well, it was as if I had put my hand in there."

"You don't think that . . . ?"

"Everything was centered on the hand, but from the hand it spread to the wrist, and from there to the forearm and the arm, and suddenly my entire body had awoken and was radiating light. And she was as well. Seconds later, I understood everything."

"What? You understood what?"

"I don't know. I've forgotten it. But I can tell you that the illumination that I experienced was so colossal that it extended back into the past and projected forward into the future. With blinding intensity it lit up my previous encounters with Mathilde and Patricia Julia, and I understood them in their totality. I remember trembling at the implications and at the full meaning of our encounters, as I understood them in the moment. If you asked me right now, I wouldn't be able to tell you what those implications were or what that meaning was, but in the moment they seemed true and transparent. I was struck by the anguish and urgency of preparing myself for possible sequels, but today I don't know what those sequels could be. They were inklings of another world that my brain has not been able to retain."

"Once again, it seems to me that you are . . ."

"But that's not all of it. The light from that beacon reached farther and lit up distant memories. I evaluated past encounters with my three lady friends from a new perspective, and I burned with embarrassment and wanted to die from my stupidity. For a few instants, which were both eternal and fleeting, I was *alive*, I was *normal*, and from that suddenly acquired normalcy I was horrified to see and identify, as though from a watchtower, the true character of my ailment. . . . Dionisio, at that moment I understood my condition, our condition; analyzing it in retrospect, I understood perfectly what was happening to me and how we trick ourselves and how the trick, the farce, is part of the zombie's curse. Of course, I have already lost this clairvoyance."

"My friend . . ."

"Wait: there's more. . . . The future opened up before me as well."

"The what?"

"Exactly! I can't explain it, but at that moment it was so very easy. . . . I saw someone who looked like me, but who wasn't precisely me, but rather who I would be later on, and this me also had plans and goals. And among all of these plans and goals one stood out, the mother of all goals that eclipsed all the others with the light of a thousand suns: I understood that the next day, the day after that, and the one after that, in all of the years to come, I wanted to be with Isadore, holding hands, just like at that moment.

Dionisio had turned thoughtful. He brooded. I harbored the hope that when he spoke again, after having listened to me for hours, he would be able to guide me and provide me with a way out of my predicament. At that moment his assistants arrived to take him away, as they always did at a particular hour of the evening. Dionisio stopped them with a gesture, and they abandoned their intentions to await further instruction. After a silence that seemed to last for centuries, Dionisio spoke.

"Did you notice if she used some sort of contraption? If she hit you with some kind of hypnotic ray?"

"No, Dionisio," I said. "No."

"Okay," he said, and made another gesture.

His grim assistants took him away.

THE FOREMAN

Every evening I sit here, *tifi*, just like Papa Vincent used to do, telling stories, and in all the time I've been doing it, I've never repeated the same story twice. For me it is a point of pride and a chance to show off, just as it was for Papa Vincent in his time. But if I had ever found myself in a tough spot, I would have repeated one of them without a second thought before I would tell this one. When I saw you arrive in your truck, get out, and start asking for me, I thought that I had gone daft. It was as if I were looking at myself from fifty years ago. I realized immediately that I had never told this story to anybody because it wasn't mine to just give away. This story is yours. When I saw you I knew that, in some way, I had trusted that one day you would come.

It's been years since anyone's seen the cashew growers. We know that they are there, but these days they aren't as numerous as before. When Old Man Sadrak died, no one took his place. At one time, rumors circulated that Ti-Placide, the foreman, was renting out his labor force to other estate owners, especially to sugar growers from Central America, in exchange for juicy percentages. It was also said that Ti-Placide periodically auctioned off his laborers to anonymous clients and that the earnings that this side business yielded far exceeded those he received from the sale of cashew nuts. Many times, too many for my own good, I watched from my hilltop as men, women, and children climbed into a truck, blindfolded, and went away, escorted by military vehicles.

Despite the decline of the neighboring village, the prohibition against visiting it or initiating friendships with its inhabitants was never lifted. Those who, over the years, dared to put our only law to the test either died beneath Sadrak's bullets or, if they were successful and jumped the fence to the other side, never returned to our village. The stupidest among them argued that those who went never came back because the cashew growers' lives were so comfortable and prosperous, not like ours, so full of suffering and miserable. They went and they didn't return, and thanks to that natural filter our humble village has always remained composed of happy people. Those of us who stay here are the ones who want to stay. When I was young, I admired the people who migrated to the city, thinking that they were running from the past, the jungle, the insects, and the agony toward civilization, fortune, prosperity, the future. Old age has corrected my perception: in that direction, beggars, garbage, overcrowding, crime; in this direction, peace, happiness, rest, magic.

We don't like cashews, but even if we did like them, we wouldn't eat them. Anyone who eats a cashew and doesn't die becomes a cashew grower, Papa Vincent used to say. Spending too much time among those plants and those people had the same effect. Forgive your father, *tifi*, if he ever treated you coldly, if he seemed inhuman or miserly on occasion. That night Pascal had the ill fortune to touch what he shouldn't have.

This story is not the only thing that I want you to take from this village. Take this. Unlike black sand, you cannot prepare white sand; it comes already made. This that you see here is all that there is in the entire world. Use it wisely. Papa Vincent told us many times that he had insisted that Placide allow him to use it on him, but Placide refused, saying that he was fine as he was. He reminded us of it to teach us an important lesson: People, in general, no matter who they are or what they do, are convinced of their own righteousness—especially the bad ones.

13. Step by Step, Day by Day / Guilt / Happiness

I feel . . . guilty. Yes. That is how I feel. Guilty. I feel guilty for not having visited Dionisio in all of this time. Guilty for having relegated my diary to oblivion. Guilty for having neglected my research.

I don't know if I am cured, surely I am not, but I know that, as Friday approaches, my thoughts are beginning to turn unruly and an electric eel making its nest in my stomach won't let up asking questions: What dress will Patricia Julia be wearing this time? How will Mathilde do her hair? What can I do to be alone with Isadore? I can barely concentrate enough to carry out my duties appropriately.

I have nothing to wear. I don't really feel like going shopping, but I don't see any other solution. I want to look good because Mathilde has promised to bring her camera next time, and I am not very photogenic to begin with. No dead person ever is.

Brainless III

Cont. transcription of the interrogation of Doctor Isadore X. Bellamy Pierre-Louis, conducted by Detectives Jaime Almánzar Soto and Reynolds Rivera Sagardí.

IB: It's easy. It doesn't fit. It doesn't have anything to do with it.

RRS: How often you repeat that sentence! "It doesn't have anything to do with it." It's your favorite sentence.

IB: Valérie was my best friend from college. Her death affected me a great deal.

RRS: Your best friends have very bad luck.

IB: Maybe the one who has bad luck is me.

RRS: That depends upon what you understand to be bad luck.

IB: To lose a loved one, Detective. To lose a loved one.

[silence]

RRS: Simònides Myrthil . . . was forty-four years old when he committed that double homicide. Retired colonel, dark complexion, green eyes, six foot three in height, his nationality was . . . well, what does his nationality matter? Right?

[silence]

RRS: Accused of human trafficking on multiple occasions, never convicted. Sentenced to thirty years in prison but transferred to the San Lázaro Psychiatric Hospital, in which he's spent ten years under minimum security. His lawyers didn't manage to get him acquitted, but the judge was convinced of his insanity and accepted the family's petition for Myrthil to carry out his sentence in a specialized facility. It was a humanitarian measure, but I am certain that the judge agreed in order to protect the prison population, not in order to placate the family. You see, Colonel Myrthil arrived home one night, just after you had left, according to your own testimony, and split his daughter Valérie and his wife Adeline's heads open with a machete. When the police arrived, the colonel was squatting over the corpses of his wife and daughter, rooting about in their skulls. According to the police report he was chewing on an encephalic mass, his mouth smeared with blood. Later, during the interrogation, the colonel explained that the people he had killed were not his wife Adeline and his daughter Valérie, but rather, mechanical imposters. He had been harboring the suspicion for months but had been growing more and more certain. That night he decided to take action. When they asked him what he was doing with the bodies of his victims when the police entered his house, he responded that he was looking for the microchips and circuits of those robotic substitutes.

IB: Detective . . .

RRS: Do you know how your best friend's father has been living for the past ten years? He spends most of his time in a padded cell. He sleeps on the floor. In the evening several robust orderlies force him into a straitjacket, cinch down all the straps so he can't move a muscle, and finally, fit a muzzle over his face so that he won't eat anybody. Only then do they take him out into the common area and sit him down behind a counter, as a protective measure. From there he watches television, receives visits from family and friends, and chats with the other nut jobs, or at least with the ones who aren't afraid to get near him. It's unlikely that they have been able to forget what happened to his first therapist, a young resident, too young and careless, if you ask me. Beautiful too . . . *before*, obviously. She insisted on treating her patient without the restrictive harnesses in the interest of giving him back his humanity, as she put it. One day the poor girl tried to explain his condition to him; she didn't leave out a single detail. She imagined—she *trusted*—that her patient would be capable of assimilating the information and actively contribute to his own treatment. The colonel, however, did not respond in the way she expected and instead tore half of her face off with his teeth.

IB: Detective . . .

RRS: The most surprising thing to me was to learn that his madness has a name!

IB: Capgras syndrome.

RRS: Capgras syndrome, exactly. If they had to put a name to it, it must be because it isn't all that rare. Let's see. . . . Because of a brain lesion or, in the case of Colonel Myrthil, intoxication by harmful substances, the temporal cortex of the brain, located in the temporal lobe and utilized in the recognition of faces, becomes disconnected from the limbic system, responsible for assigning emotions to stimuli and memories. In this way the person suffering from Capgras syndrome can physically recognize the face of a loved one without that stimulus provoking the ordinary emotional reaction assigned to that recognition. Are you following me, Doctor? Is my language too abstruse?

IB: The brain is an incredible organ, capable of many things except self-diagnosis. It perceives the incongruence, it knows that something is off, but it never assigns responsibility to itself.

RRS: Very good! It never assigns responsibility to itself. What it does is whisper a possible explanation to the conscious self. Put another way, it invents a story. I imagine that in Colonel Myrthil's case it went more or less like this: Now every time I see my wife and daughter I don't feel any of the things that I used to feel when I saw them; if I don't feel what I remember feeling every time I used to see them, it means that they are not my real wife and daughter. If they are not my real wife and daughter, they must be imposters. It's all downhill from there.

IB: So it is.

RRS: The limbic system. . . . Help me here, Doctor. I'm forgetting some of my medical forensics lessons, you know? From when I got my master's degree.

IB: The limbic system is made up of the hypothalamus and the amygdala.

RRS: The amygdala . . . just a moment. . . . The amygdala! I'm certain that this isn't the first time you've mentioned that word during our conversation. Jaime, am I correct?

[Detective Almánzar Soto looks through his notes.]

JAS: "The compound he was trying to stabilize was intended to adhere to the dendrites of the cerebral amygdala and restore the polarity of the axoplasm."

RSS: Yes! I knew it! It's curious, don't you think? Your beloved boss was trying to invent a medicine that might have been able to help the colonel . . . a formula that could have defibrillated his brain, as you put it.

IB: That is absurd!

RRS: Why? Anyway, it had to be tested on someone.

IB: What are you saying? What makes you think that that deranged man and my . . . ?

[A brief, dry sound, like a slap, interrupts Doctor Bellamy. Detective Rivera Sagardí has dropped a thick ream of papers on the desk.]

RRS: Dionisio, to his friends.

[Doctor Bellamy leafs through the manuscript in silence.]

RRS: We had a search warrant. Pretty handwriting, don't you think? And the binding is . . . what can I say? Worthy of a masterpiece. We found it in the study in his house, very beautiful, of course, very . . . functional. Apparently the doctor already had a ritual every Friday. You and your friends stole the colonel's most frequent visitor.

[Doctor Bellamy reads, slack-jawed.]

RRS: But you are correct. To insinuate that the deceased frequented the San Lázaro Psychiatric Hospital and that he had struck up a friendship with its most dangerous inmate with the sole objective of corroborating the effectiveness of his concoctions . . . well, what can I tell you? It's pure speculation. He could just as easily have ingested them himself to see if they worked or not. . . . In fact, I don't doubt that he would have done so, if you ask me.

[There are tears on Doctor Bellamy's face.]

RRS: You see, the top scientist that you and your friends keep crying over was crazier than a goat. . . . Yes! Well, at least crazier than the colonel. Completely harmless, but definitely crazier, in my opinion. Heir to an immeasurable fortune, but afflicted for the past twenty years with Cotard's syndrome. Are you familiar with it? It's worse even than Capgras: a whole other turn of the screw . . . or two. The difference between the one and the other is that the emotional disconnect doesn't only affect the recognition of loved ones' faces— the emotional disconnect affects the recognition of absolutely everything, *including one's own self.* The story that the brain invents to explain the situation? "I must be dead and rotting."

[Doctor Bellamy has stopped reading.]

RRS: His parents, dead, . . . actually dead. No siblings or close relatives. His monthly income was controlled by executors who disbursed the funds under the condition that the beneficiary could provide evidence that he was attending a weekly therapy session, as stipulated in the will. We are talking about a lot of money. Five Fridays ago he stopped attending.

[Doctor Bellamy cries.]

RRS: His appointment was not with one specific therapist but rather with a veritable battery of doctors, all paid from a trust fund designated by his parents. We have spoken with several of them, but it wasn't really necessary in order to know, after even a cursory read through these pages, that the madness this man was subsumed in was impenetrable. Not content with having provided him with an impossible alibi, his brain had fabricated a baroque tangle of nonsense taken from horror films. He saw everything through the lens of his fantasy, like Don Quixote. He was a zombie. The colonel as well, and many others who live among us, walking on eggshells lest we discover them, including the guard who killed him. The medicines that he needed to take were exotic products that made it easier to camouflage. The common area in the insane asylum was a tavern presided over by Dionisio, where he, and others like him, went to talk and to share their unfathomable torments, pursued by mysterious organizations. . . . Pure paranoid entelechy. Very tragic. . . .

[Doctor Bellamy blows her nose.]

RRS: But, as I've already told you, that's a whole other kettle of fish. This case is closed. I suppose we will just have to be satisfied with wishing we understood. We still need to speak with Miss Cáceres. We have been calling her. If you speak with her, please tell her that we are waiting for her here.

[A chair slides. Doctor Bellamy stands up.]

RRS: He was on the verge of curing himself, you know? Without miracle brews. It was impossible, because of his condition, for him to figure out what the secret ingredient was that was missing from his concoction. But, as you see, the old proverb must be true: sometimes the cure is worse than the disease.

[Doctor Bellamy hands the manuscript back to Detective Rivera Sagardí.]

RRS: Keep it. We made a copy especially for you. I recommend chapter twelve. It's my favorite.

[Heels move away. A door opens and closes again. The interview ends.]

14. Get Up and Come Out

Lazarus must have felt something similar when Jesus ordered him to get up, to come out. Suddenly you abandon the dark, the confinement, the stench; your lungs fill with pure air that smells like a woman's fine perfume, and all of your bronchioles get to their feet for a standing ovation; your muscles regain their elasticity, and your skin flushes with a heat that frightens off the cold . . . but I can't see anything.

Am I still underground? Am I still encased in my coffin? No. I never was. I'm standing. I can move, but I don't want to move. Now soft hands caress my face and unknot the blindfold that covers my eyes. In front of me, three angels. Or perhaps only one? A single tripartite presence. One of them, any one of them, approaches me and pokes about in my ears, in which buzzes the persistent echo of an explosion. She returns to her place and I realize that, until that moment, I had been deaf.

I had eyes and I couldn't see. I had ears and I couldn't hear. I was a stone in the water, dry inside. But they took matters into their own hands.

The sounds of the world reach me. I find myself in a lovely apartment, flooded with clear light filtered through bamboo curtains. I am surrounded by books, splendid paintings, mysterious figurines, idols from civilizations lost in time. Have I been here before? They look from one to the other, but they do not speak. The one in the middle of the other two is holding a diminutive remote control in her hands. An idol that I recognize. She presses a button. From everywhere and nowhere surges a sad melody overlaid with a happy voice singing a pleasant song about thwarted love. Is it the first time that I've heard it? It doesn't matter. It's the most beautiful thing that I've ever heard. They smile and approach me. They take me by the hand, they lead me, and I follow them. I know that I will be fine wherever it is that they take me. I'm overcome by a sensation of supreme well-being.

Spineless

Transcription of the interrogation of Miss Patricia Julia Cáceres Singüenza, conducted by Detectives Jaime Almánzar Soto and Reynolds Rivera Sagardí.

JAS: Good morning.

PJC: What's so good about it?

RRS: Have a seat, please.

PJC: I prefer to remain standing. Tell me what you want to know, and I will tell you if you can know it or not.

JAS: Could I offer you a little . . .

PJC: There's nothing you could offer me that I'd want. This is what the police are really very good at, harassing innocent citizens. That night, tell me, that night when a good man died, a man whom the two of you could never equal, even standing one on top of the other, that night, where were the police?

RRS: Miss, I'll remind you that . . .

PJC: I am a licensed professional, thank you very much; you do not need to remind me of anything. In any case, I'm the one who has to remind you two that dead people don't bury themselves, although some imbeciles might believe that they walk and talk and go to the movies.

RRS: What on earth are you talking about?

PJC: You heard me perfectly well. Doctor Bellamy already caught me up on how you treated her and on the string of slander that you heaped on top of our boss. And not to even mention what you must have done to Mathilde, who called me in the middle of the morning in a sea of tears.

JAS: We didn't . . .

PJC: You didn't what? Perhaps you imagined that there'd be no one to mourn this dead man, right? That it was just another body recovered by the police from a ditch along the seawall or somewhere in the cane fields. Well, you are mistaken. And now, if you'll excuse me, I have a lot of things to take care of.

RRS: Miss Cáceres, you know very well that the hospital must turn the body over to us for the autopsy.

PJC: In your dreams. Don't think for a single second that I'm going to allow you to lay a hand on him and then return him to me with those stitches up his chest. You're crazy.

JAS: It's the law.

PJC: Then arrest me. Do you really think that I came all the way over here without having consulted with the company's attorneys?

[There is a dry sound. Miss Cáceres has deposited a dossier upon the desk. Detective Almánzar leafs through it. It contains orders from a civil court.]

PCJ: The body will remain with us. In fact, we are already moving it to the funeral home.

RRS: But . . .

PJC: These interrogations are finished. I know very well why you are so interested in the matter; I'm not swallowing this story of yours about "helping the public prosecutor to strengthen his case." Give me a break. . . .

JAS: We just want to do our jobs.

PJC: Tell that to your partner, who hasn't once stopped staring at my legs.

[Detective Rivera coughs. Miss Cáceres opens the door to leave.]

PJC: And one more thing . . .

RRS: Go ahead.

PJC: I am leaving here with copies of all of these interviews, including the one we are having right now, so go and tell the stenographer.

RRS: And why do you need them?

PJC: They're ours by law. Our lawyers are exploring what kind of legal action to take against you, and they need a foundation to build their case on. But to tell you the truth, I really want them for Doctor Bellamy. I am certain that she'll find a place for them in her scrapbook. She's like that. Good afternoon, gentlemen.

[Miss Cáceres leaves. The interview ends.]

APPENDIX

Glossary of Wicked Weeds

The following are excerpts from Isadore Bellamy's scrapbook. A warning to the curious, but inexpert reader: do not handle any of these plants, much less combine them.

Bresillet. The *Comocladia glabra* tree is detested by rural folk. It is extremely difficult to eradicate. In these places the notion persists that in order to really kill something (so that it won't return, so that it won't come back to life), it is necessary to burn it. Brush piles are burned, along with hives, anthills, termite nests—but not the bresillet: the smoke it produces is exceedingly dangerous. It causes delirium and sudden death. The sap from this tree is toxic and causes dermatitis and severe inflammation. Popular wisdom has issued its edict, of course, in order to protect the children: the bresillet is a tree sown by the devil, and anyone who climbs it will be promptly strangled by its branches and devoured.

Bwa pine. *Zanthoxylum martinicense* is a plant possessing narcotic effects. Rural Jamaicans use its bark to prepare an infusion that cures syphilis. Chewing the bark alleviates toothache but produces hallucinations. The young roots may also be used to make a broth that kills parasites, although it should be taken only by those who can tolerate its psychedelic effects.

Calmador. The leaves of *Dieffenbachia seguine* contain calcium oxalate crystals. These crystals damage tissue at the cellular level, irritating it and causing inflammation. Its common name is pure irony.

Consigne. In Cuba and Haiti *Trichilia hirta* is used to make infusions that cure anemia, asthma, bronchitis, and pneumonia. It is also used in the magical-religious rituals of the Yoruba and Bakongo cults. Some African tribes use the plant to induce vomiting. Its use as a suppository can cause serious neurological damage. Excessive doses are generally fatal.

Frou-frou. A fish is not a plant, but without the venom from the frou-frou, blowfish, or puffer fish, none of the plants cataloged here will yield the desired effect. In a certain sense, frou-frou venom provides the catalytic converter that induces the zombie state. This substance, known as tetrodotoxin, is one of the most potent poisons on the planet. A single fish contains enough to kill thirty people. Curiously, the toxin is not produced by the fish itself, but rather by bacteria that maintain a symbiotic relationship with the fish. Two varieties of frou-frou are used: *Canthigaster punctatissimus* and *Arothron meleagris*. The toxin from the first, extracted and then cooked, dyes the mixture black. The second dyes it white. No one has been able to tell me if the effects differ between the two. In the villages along the southern coast (Jacmel, Port Salut, Aquin) the dried corpses of the frou-frou are made into attractive lamps.

Malpitte. *Datura stramonium* is one of the best known and most infamous of all wicked weeds. It goes by multiple names: jimson weed, devil's trumpet, angel's trumpet, devil's seed, crazy hat, mad tea, devil's breadbasket, Korean morning glory, loco weed, augushka, and zombie pickle. It belongs to the solanaceae (nightshade) family, plants that are extensively used by man. Potatoes, paprika, tomatoes, eggplant, chilies, and petunias are members of this group. But so are mandrake, tobacco, and belladonna (deadly nightshade), principal components of innumerable spells and curses.

Malpitte is seriously respected by rural folk, and with good reason. This plant practically drips tropane alkaloids. Ingesting it in any form is a guarantee of delirium, possibly permanent. Its active ingredients are the anticholinergics atropine, hyoscyamine, and scopolamine. According to tradition, this plant is the only thing that a zombie should eat in order to avoid "ripening."

Mashasha. *Dalechampia scandens* is a wicked little member of the stinging nettle family. Touching the plant and screaming are synonymous. On contact, the urticant trichomes rupture, and the fluid stored in their bases is injected into the epidermis. This fluid contains acetylcholine (a neurotransmitter), 5-hydroxytryptamine (a monoamine), and histamines—a formula of serotonins that are like the ABCs of pain. It causes itching, swelling, and stinging, but also hallucinations and the distinctive out-of-body sensation of shamanic experiences (triggered, no doubt, by free tryptamines).

Morivivi. *Mimosa pudica* is a perennial creeping weed in the Fabaceae family that, when touched, closes its bipinnate leaves. It is also known as bashful plant and sleeping grass. The morivivi is a plant and a metaphor all in one, and it is one of the few pantropical plants described in Ayurvedic medicine. Its flower, a spherical bloom, is used to combat insomnia.

Pois grater. This climbing vine, a species of *Mucuna*, contains psychoactive substances. The fruit it produces is covered in trichomes (fine surface hairs) that cause severe itching due to an enzyme called mucunain. The trichomes also contain substances that trigger the release of histamines, very similar to those found in bee and snake venom. Weeds are Nature's encyclopedia.

Pomme-cajou. The cashew tree, *Anacardium occidentale*, belongs to the poison ivy family. The raw cashew is very poisonous. Brushing against any part of the plant causes inflam-

mation of the skin owing to substances such as cardol, ana-
cardic acid, anacardol, and cardanol. The cashew seed is one
of the most expensive nuts in the world, surpassed only by
the macadamia. The largest producer of cashew nuts is Viet-
nam, followed by Nigeria, India, and Brazil; they have a
combined production of one million tons.

Pringamoza. *Urera baccifera*, also known as mala mujer, ortiga
brava, and pica-pica, belongs to the stinging nettle family. It
is widely used to treat problems related to menstruation:
amenorrhea, inflammation of the ovaries, spanomenorrhea,
and blennorrhea. Some highly experienced healers use it in
any case that requires the movement of blood from one place
to another. Its components are like sheepdogs to hemoglo-
bin.

Tcha-tcha. The tcha-tcha, or *Albizia lebbeck*, belongs to the
leguminous plant family. Its pharmacological activity is
comprised of a group of glycosides known as saponins.
Despite the fact that the majority of saponins can be absorbed
by the intestine, for countless generations folk culture has
preferred topical application. I never saw Sandrine use the
plant in any other way, and with good reason. The symptoms
of poisoning from the saponins contained in the tcha-tcha
include nausea, vomiting, abundant secretions in respiratory
passages, and pulmonary edema. A fatal dose causes the victim to choke on his own fluids. He literally melts to death.
The tcha-tcha also contains a strange saponin called a sapo-
toxin that interferes with cellular respiration in all parts of
the body (simultaneously) and induces death by impairing
all vital functions.

About the Author

Pedro Cabiya is a poet, screenwriter and award-winning author of the bestselling novels *Trance* and *The Head,* as well as the seminal short-story collections *Historias tremendas* (Pen Club Book of the Year) and *Historias atroces.* His work has been featured in numerous international anthologies, and his open letters, opinion pieces and essays on politics, religion, human rights, art and science regularly become viral phenomena. He has lived in Spain, the United States, Haiti and Puerto Rico. He currently resides in the Dominican Republic, where he is Dean of Academic Affairs at the American School of Santo Domingo and Senior Producer at Heart of Gold Films. Follow him @PedroCabiya and www.pedrocabiya.com.